D1368151

190003

Country Music

**Center Point
Large Print**

**This Large Print Book carries the
Seal of Approval of N.A.V.H.**

Country Music

Jane Candia Coleman

CENTER POINT PUBLISHING
THORNDIKE, MAINE

This Center Point Large Print edition is published in the year 2006 by arrangement with Golden West Literary Agency.

The text of this Large Print edition is unabridged. In other aspects, this book may vary from the original edition. Printed in Thailand.
Set in 16-point Times New Roman type.

ISBN 1-58547-742-7

Library of Congress Cataloging-in-Publication Data

Coleman, Jane Candia.
    Country music / Jane Candia Coleman.--Center Point large print ed.
      p. cm.
    ISBN 1-58547-742-7 (lib. bdg. : alk. paper)
      1. Large type books. 2. Western stories. I. Title.

PS3553.O47427C68 2006
813'.54--dc22
                                                    2005029053

TABLE OF CONTENTS

Foreword   7
The Silence of Snow   11
Renegade Trail   30
Aunt Addy and the Cattle Rustler   84
The *Paseo*   99
Simple Amy   109
China Doll   120
Sunflower   133
Holy Water   148
For Two Dollars   162
Learning the Names of Things   180
Country Music   202

Foreword

Several years ago my mother asked me where I got "all the ideas" for short stories.

"Do you want the short course or the long one?" I asked in response.

"The short one."

"Good," I said, because explaining something as nebulous as the kernel of a story on a long distance call would have taken hours.

So I gave the simplest answer. "I don't know."

We both laughed.

The truth, however, is that stories are everywhere if one looks for them—in history books, folklore, newspapers, snatches of conversation, people glimpsed in passing, simple curiosity.

For years I had wondered about Janette Riker, the young girl forced by tragic circumstance to spend a bitter winter alone in the Rocky Mountains. What was it like? What thoughts were hers? To satisfy my curiosity, I wrote "The Silence of Snow."

"Renegade Trail" had its beginning in a few lines of history about a horse drive from Texas to Nebraska. As a horse lover, I was interested to discover the differences between driving a large number of horses and driving cattle. I had learned, however, when writing my cattle drive novel, *The O'Keefe Empire*, that stories about cows are not of interest unless the focus is on people, so "Renegade Trail" took a different direction, with characters and plot taking center stage.

"Aunt Addy and the Cattle Rustler" began with a photograph of a tough, old Cochise County, Arizona homesteader—a woman who raised a large family and became a prosperous rancher after being deserted by her husband.

"The *Paseo*" had its beginnings when a New Mexican woman mentioned to me that, when a child, a local painter asked to do her portrait, and as a consequence was driven out of town by the horrified older women who suspected that he wanted to do more than paint her face. This is his story.

The Lee boys of Paradise, Arizona were famous in the 'Twenties and 'Thirties for their lion hunting ability and their fine hounds. When I heard that they'd named a lion the dogs couldn't track "Simple Amy," after the famous Aimee Semple McPherson, well, who could resist a story about her and her reappearance after being missing for several months? Not I. The fact that she walked over the border from Agua Prieta into Douglas, Arizona—where I do my shopping—only added to the fun.

I have also long been fascinated by the Chinese who came to America to build railroads, to better themselves and their families, and to find "Gold Mountain." The characters in "China Doll" are all based on fact, as is, of course, the underlying story of the gunfight at the O.K. Corral. It is worthy of note that, while Wyatt Earp and his friends and enemies have become household words, the Chinese citizens of Tombstone have for the most part been overlooked and forgotten. Pity.

Every city and town has a Susannah and a Clay, good and bad marriages. Because I am a believer in happy endings, "Sunflower" ends, if not ecstatically, then true to at least some lives and far better than it did in actuality.

"Holy Water" is a story that could only happen in the West, where water is both sacred and vital. As in the 19th century, fights over water in whatever form continue into the present and not always wisely.

For the past thirty-five years I have been collecting Indian pottery, baskets, rugs, jewelry. My fascination with these art forms has its roots in a duality—love of earth and fascination with the creative process. "For Two Dollars" was inspired by master potter María Martínez, but is not in any way her story. Rather, it is the story of an artist chosen, blessed, seeking a way to shape her visions.

Because of climate, the Southwest is home to many homeless. Who are they? Curiosity led me to investigate a camp in the brush, and then to write "Learning the Names of Things," using bits and pieces of people I have known. There really is a Loper, bless him, a Jim Turtle, and a Hippie, although they will never recognize themselves in their new rôles with new names, and the Hippie is, of course, illiterate.

To come full circle, I can't say where "Country Music" began. It wove itself and its themes out of people, landscape, simple joys, and actual tragedies— out of war, the tragedy of many illegal aliens in the

Southwest, ancient rituals, and healing. To say this story was a "given" sounds simplistic, but is close to the truth.

Although all stories are about people, it is the Western landscape that inspires me, that is, in itself, a character, that, in its magnificence, its harshness, its justice has shaped those of us who live here, and those whose stories I have chosen to tell.

Jane Candia Coleman

The Silence of Snow

"I am alone." I say the words out loud to break the silence, but they only make it deeper, a white shroud.

"I am alone."

Not even an echo answers. A raven flies in the distance, too far away for me to hear the sound of his wings. He is as black as the snow is dazzling white.

How long has it been since Pa and Jacky rode off and left me? I've lost track of days. At first I went out and searched for them, but then I realized they were gone, swallowed up by this country that seems to have no end and no beginning.

The three of us were on our way to Oregon. I see now it was foolish to try it without the company of others, but that was always Pa's way. He worked best by himself and never could learn to take orders from anybody.

"Independent as a hog on ice" was how Ma put it. She was the only person who could talk sense into him, but then she died, and I think Pa couldn't stand the home place without her.

He never asked Jacky or me our feelings about what he decided, just sold the farm and announced we were leaving for Oregon. We didn't argue. His mind was made up, and after a few days on the trail we began to think of it as a great adventure.

It was—then. We'd never been more than ten miles away from where we were born, and it was exciting, moving across the plains, seeing buffalo—so many they covered the prairie like a dark blanket as far as I could see.

There were other people on the trail, of course, and sometimes we camped with them when there was an Indian scare. On those nights Jacky and I talked with the kids our age and, once in a while, got to join in the games and dancing. Pa would talk to the other men or the wagon master, or to the troops of soldiers riding between forts. All in all, I never noticed the silence what with the creak of wheels, the sound of hoofs, and the wind that seemed to blow all the time. Not until now.

We'd gotten as far as this valley by late September, and Pa decided to stop and feed up the oxen and horses before trying to cross the mountains. I thought it was a pretty place with plenty of cured grass and the trees on the lower slopes turning red and gold. We set up camp against a little rise, and Jacky and I turned out the oxen and went to look around and gather firewood.

"I wonder what it would be like living here," I remember I said.

He laughed. "Oregon's better."

"How do you know? You've never been there." I figured he was thinking about a girl he'd danced with one night who was headed there with her family.

"We haven't passed anything like a town in a month," he said. "That's not my idea of living."

Jacky is, or was, nineteen and restless. It wouldn't be long before he got himself a bride. Then it would be my turn.

Only now I'm not sure of anything, not even tomorrow. I'm talking to myself and to this journal just to keep from letting go. There are times I've felt it would be better to lie down in the snow and shut my eyes and leave this world. But the voice inside won't let me. It nags and bosses, and I listen to it because it's the only voice, aside from my own, that I hear.

That night we were almost out of meat, but Pa had seen fresh buffalo sign, so he and Jacky went off early the next morning, leaving me in camp. I wasn't afraid. There was an old rifle and a shotgun in the wagon, and I'd been using both since I was big enough to hold them steady.

"Keep that fire going," Pa told me. "I can taste that meat already."

I waved. "Me, too."

That was the last I saw of them, two men on horseback, disappearing into the trees along the creek where the falling leaves turned the air pure gold.

There was wash to get done, and, once I had the clothes spread out to dry, I turned out our beds, shook the quilts, and swept the wagon. One thing I'd learned on the trail was to take advantage of any lay-over and get done what was needed, because you didn't know when you'd get a chance again.

Roanie, my little horse, kept me company while I did chores. Sometimes he acts more like a dog, but that doesn't fool me. Like Pa always said: "As soon as you get to thinking he's a puppy, he'll pull some stunt and kill you."

Anyhow, I talked to him, and once in a while he snorted and blew at me, and all in all I didn't have time to notice night was coming on. Not till my stomach told me I'd forgotten to eat.

I built up the fire and put on the kettle of beans and salt pork. Pa and Jacky would be back and hungry, and, with luck, they'd have a buffalo hump and tongue or even an antelope. We'd seen plenty of them in the last weeks.

The sun disappeared behind the mountains, and with it any warmth. I pulled on a jacket and gathered the dry clothes and noticed the scent of frost in the air.

Where were they? Worry nagged at me, kept me pacing, kept my hands moving for something to take my mind off the fact that it was dark and I might have been the only person alive in the whole world. I piled more wood on the fire in hopes it would act like a beacon, and then thought, if there were Indians around, they'd see it, too. That scared me, but I decided to take the chance. I leaned against the wheel of the wagon and watched the flames, saw the sparks rise up like tiny, red stars against black sky.

"Bring them back," I prayed. "Please, bring Pa and Jacky home."

By morning the fire had burned low, and I was still alone—just me and Roanie and the oxen asleep in the meadow. For breakfast I ate the rest of the beans before saddling Roanie. I figured Pa or Jacky was hurt somewhere and depending on me.

Their trail was easy to follow at first. It led through a

little stand of trees, and then across another creek into a stretch of rocks that made it harder, but there were tracks here and there and still fresh manure. I followed down a gully and up over the steep side onto prairie. It was empty as far as I could see, and that was far—and nothing but yellow grass and the sky coming down around like a blue cup.

Out there the wind was strong and cold, and had a taste in it like snow. The prairie was big and empty with just me sitting there alone. I pulled my jacket closer, and then started to cry and couldn't stop, even when Roanie curved his neck around and nudged my boot like he was asking what was the matter.

When hopelessness hits you smack in the face, it's hard to keep from crying. And sitting out there on the edge of that place, I knew what I was doing was hopeless. Whatever had happened, I'd never know. I was on my own with nobody for a thousand miles to help or console me for the loss of my whole family.

Despair creeps up in stages. After that first time, it gets worse with every chore, and it keeps you awake at night, wondering, imagining things worse than any nightmare, asking questions that have no answers. Somewhere Pa was hurt, maybe dead, and my brother, too. That's what's hard. That's what leaves you with an ache that doesn't go away, not even when morning comes.

I rode out for three days, riding wide circles, looking for sign that wasn't there. What I found was prairie, brush-filled gullies, deep cañons that split the mountains apart as if God had come down with an axe and cracked the rock open.

On the evening of the third day the snow started, a few flakes at first, and then heavier so the fire sizzled and smoked and finally died down to a few coals. Out of habit, I scooped them into a metal bucket and took it inside the wagon with me. Then I spent another night picturing all the different ways to die.

Get those shirt tails cracking, girl! You've got work to do! The voice was unfamiliar, but it came from inside my head.

"Leave me be," I said, wishing I could close my eyes and sleep.

I won't. Use your wits, and stop acting like a baby.

"I'm not!"

You are. Lying around crying, instead of figuring how you're going to get out of this.

"I'll never." The thought lay on me heavy as the snow.

Your pa didn't raise a quitter.

"Pa's dead."

And you aren't.

That was the truth. I looked out and saw Roanie, coming up from the creek. Icicles dripped from his nose, and snow had balled in his hoofs so he walked carefully. What would happen to him if I wasn't here? He might survive, but then again. . . . The thought of him brought down by wolves was awful. And then there were the oxen with their velvet eyes that I'd named the

16

day we set out for Oregon. Matthew, Mark, Luke, and John. I figured with names like that, they'd surely get us all where we were going.

It seemed I was responsible—for them and for me. Me, Janette Riker, sixteen years old come December if I lived that long. I guessed I had to give it a try.

The day warmed up, and the snow melted. For a long time I sat figuring what I had to do, and what to do first, and that almost made me want to die all over again.

"I can't," I said.

Just get to work came the answer.

The wagon sat where we'd put it, at an angle on the east side of the rise, but it wouldn't be enough to keep me from freezing when the real winter came. If I put up a shelter, I'd make it against the hill, with a pen for Roanie between it and the wagon. That way we'd both be protected, north and east, from the wind and snow.

I looked at the wood Jacky and I had dragged in. There was plenty of it, and plenty more by the creek and at the base of the mountains, and some of the logs were good size. In the wagon were Pa's shovels, saws, and axes—all the tools he figured he'd be using on a new place. Pa's fiddle was in there, too, the one he played for dances or around the fire when we were camped for the night. Remembering those times—Pa with his eyes half shut, making music that wrapped you in a kind of bright spell—made my tears come again.

Oh, I cried a lot that day and the next as I cut and hauled wood from everywhere, and once almost hacked off my own foot. If I hadn't been quick, I'd have done

17

it and bled to death, and, though I thought I wanted to die, when faced with it, I got scared and cried harder, until there weren't any tears left. But there was work, from the time I got up until I fell into bed after dark.

I used Roanie to haul the biggest logs, though he didn't take to it right away and had to be taught a lesson with a willow whip. That hurt me more than him. I'd never hit a horse in my life, but I'd never been desperate, either.

At the end of a week, I had a stack of logs and poles higher than my head, and a hunger that wouldn't let go. I'd been living on beans and corn cakes, but I needed meat—the meat Pa and Jacky had gone out to get.

Roanie and I went out to the prairie where the antelope were so tame it was almost sinful to shoot one. My first shot missed, I can't say why, there were so many it seemed the earth was moving, rippling with maybe a thousand of the critters. With the next, I brought down a buck and set about skinning and gutting him, and trying not to look into his eyes. I never was one for killing, but I realized, kneeling out there on the ground with the blood and guts on my hands, that I wanted to live, and, if that meant killing, so be it.

Maybe I needed that lesson. Maybe up till then I'd been playing a game with half a heart. It seems so now, months and several killings later.

At first Roanie objected to having the carcass tied on the saddle, and for the second time I lost my temper and hollered.

"Damned dumb horse! You have to help. It's just us

18

out here. All we've got is us, see?" Then I kicked him in the ribs.

No sense telling about the look in his eyes. I was changing, and he couldn't understand. I changed a lot more since. Anybody knowing me back home wouldn't recognize me. Not wearing Jacky's work pants held up with rope, they wouldn't. I've never seen a woman wearing pants in all my life, but to do what I've been doing, a dress only gets in the way. Besides, mine fell apart, and I used the rags to help stuff the cracks between the logs of my house, that and the tules and moss I carted back from the creek.

Nothing went easily, but the snow held off after that first time. I got the poles dug into the ground, and banked dirt all around, then stretched a spare canvas for a roof. After that I pushed and hauled and shoved the little stove we'd brought inside, and thought I was done. Except then I realized I needed wood in order to fire it up.

"More wood!" My voice sounded puny and brought home the fact that I'd got the habit of talking to myself.

More wood! More wood! The echo inside was making fun of my complaint. *Get out there and start chopping!*

"Go to hell." I've learned to cuss somewhere during my labors. Who's going to tell me no? Besides, it feels good, makes me forget the pain from splinters in my hands, torn and bloody fingernails, blistered heels, the hunger in my belly, and makes Roanie straighten up and take notice whenever he gets sulky which isn't too often any more. He didn't even spook the morning I went down to the meadow to slaughter Matthew. It was cold. The kind of cold that sits on your shoulders and freezes your backbone, and there was a mean wind out of the east. I thought it was going to snow hard, and that it was time to do what I'd been putting off.

The old rifle weighed heavy in my hands, and the walk down through the dried grass took twice as long. Matthew looked at me out of those purple-brown eyes that seemed to know everything, and for just that moment I hated myself, and what I was going to do.

Somebody told me that the Indians ask forgiveness of the animals they hunt and kill for food, so I asked his just before I pulled the trigger and he went down.

It's hard work, skinning and gutting an ox. Finally I had to go back to the house for the axe so I could lop off the hoofs and head, chop through the bones of the hindquarters. If there was anything delicate about me when I started, it was wiped clean out by the time I got the meat up on Roanie and started back.

That night the wolves came. I hoped they'd stay in the meadow, howling and growling over what was left of Matthew. The wind had died down, and I didn't know such cold could happen. My face ached with it, even next to the stove and wearing all the clothes I could put on and still walk. I sat on Ma's chair, holding the rifle and wondering if those wolves would come up and try to jump Roanie.

There's times you feel so small your mind closes down and you can't even pray. I stayed awake all night.

The snow started just when night was lifting. If the wolves were still there, I couldn't tell through the storm, and I didn't dare leave to find out for fear I'd not find my way back.

It snowed for three days, and I was nearly buried alive. Once or twice I went out as far as the little corral to check on Roanie. He had his tail to the wind and was standing as close as he could get to the wall next to the stove. I couldn't stand knowing he was freezing, and went in and hauled out one of the quilts to strap over him. At the sight of me holding that quilt blowing in the wind, he spooked good and skittered around in the pen a long while before he'd let me near him. Even then, every time I'd get it across his back the wind would blow harder and I had to start all over again. By the time I got it tied down, I was afraid my hands were frostbit.

You're a damned fool! The voice was scolding me as I crouched by the stove, trying to get some feeling back in my fingers.

I knew that. Without the use of my hands I might as well give up. Hands, feet, a clear head, those were the things that counted. I couldn't afford to lose any one of them.

I was lucky. And I learned a lesson. For the next three days I stayed in, scraping the ox hide that I needed for a door. It would be better than the piece of canvas that didn't do much to keep out the wind, or the snow, either.

It smelled bad for a while, but I got used to that.

You'd be surprised what you can get used to. If I get through this winter, I'll never be the same again. Maybe I'll even change my name. Oh, I think about silly things like that when I have time to think. Like how it would feel to get clean again all over; I must stink as bad as that ox hide. Or like how I'd love an apple pie full of cinnamon and sweet as sugar. My mouth crinkles up so I have to spit, and the voice warns me.

Quit making yourself miserable!

I'm not. I've got this far, so maybe I'll make it till spring. Maybe somebody will come along and find me. Miracles do happen. The Bible says so. I've been reading Ma's Bible off and on, and it makes sense to me, at least out here where God's work is everywhere I look.

There are days when the sun dances on the snow, strikes red out of the brush by the creek, and the trees lay down purple shadows, and it seems like somebody's been out with a paint brush just making a picture. Days like that, the mountains rise up like white church steeples clear to the blue sky, and all around is the silence that's as loud as the wind that comes with storms. It's like the world was just made, and God hasn't decided to create the noisy things like people and animals yet.

Then Roanie stamps in his little pen. He wants to get out and see if he can't find something to eat. Winter's been hard on him, but there's not much I can do about it except let him out to eat tree bark and paw for the old grass under the snow.

I guess I'm pretty sorry-looking, too, not that it matters. There's no one to see. I wish there was.

Another of those blizzards that never seem to end. And now I find that Mark, Luke, and John must've drifted off, and that's the end of what I figured would keep me in meat.

In the damned whiteness, nothing moves. I flounder around like a minnow on a hook, and all there is around me is emptiness. Where did the antelope go? The deer? How can anybody live in a place without movement or sound, and why should I try?

Eve in the garden couldn't compare with me. She had Adam and apples. I have one poor horse and some mostly empty sacks of meal and beans, and I've boiled Matthew's bones so much there's nothing left of them. Nowhere do I hear the voice of the Almighty telling me I'm saved.

It must be getting close to spring. The nights don't have that awful cold, like being sunk in the bottom of a well, and the sun comes up earlier. Roanie's hair is shedding. Under his winter coat he's skin and bone, but at least he's gotten through the worst part. Pretty soon there should be some grass for him.

For me, I'm not sure. This morning I ate the last of the meat from Matthew. What's left is cornmeal and half a sack of beans. Once that's gone, I'm not sure what will happen, but maybe I'll be able to get out and hunt or, at least, set some rabbit snares. I see their tracks now and again, little pointy markings on top of the snow.

I'm hungry right now. Can almost smell that apple pie I keep dreaming about. Ma made the best pies I ever ate out of whatever was in season—berries, plums, the little, stunted cherries that grew in the woods. It seems like a hundred years ago, and her still alive, and Pa, coming in from the field, his sleeves rolled up, his hair wet and slicked back, saying: "Hope you made one for yourself. This one's mine."

That time won't ever come again. When I think like that, my heart jumps around and bangs in my throat. Why did this happen? What's going to happen next?

There's mud everywhere. The floor of this house is mud up past my ankles, and more keeps coming in the door. I'm worn out trying to shovel it. Give me snow. It doesn't weigh as much and stays where it's put!

My woodpile is all wet, and I can't get a fire going. It just smokes and fills up the room, and I'm wet, dirty, colder than I've been all winter. The snow may be thawing, but it's still cold out, and everything is gray and brown, and soaked through.

Still hungry. I ate the last of the beans yesterday—raw because there wasn't any way to cook them. I just soaked them till they got soft enough to chew. Now I've got cramps that won't quit and no place to lie down that's dry.

After all I've done, I feel helpless, like I'm at the end of my tether. Maybe I should have let go and died months ago, because what's it come to? What was the use?

Today I took a shot at a pack rat that was coming out of the wagon. I missed. Too weak to hold the rifle steady. Ate a handful of cornmeal and a cup of melted snow water, but can't make it much longer.

There's the horse.

The voice is the voice of evil. I put my hands over my ears but can't blot it out. "Not Roanie! I raised him from the time he was born."

Suit yourself.

I keep thinking that, when winter's over, I'll need him to get me some place—if he can carry me. If before that he lays down and dies, that's different. But right now he's all the family I have left, and how can I explain that to myself or to the damned voice of reason?

Little fool.

"He's all I've got." That's the truth. He's warm and friendly, and we're in this together. Everybody needs a friend, even if it's just a dumb animal. And I need one most of all.

Maybe there's a rabbit caught in one of the snares. Maybe. My mouth waters so bad thinking about it, I almost choke. Thinking about shooting Roanie makes me choke twice as bad.

I took to sleeping in the wagon. At least it was dry inside, though the wheels had sunk down in the mud so the whole floor was at a slant.

Mornings I woke light-headed, hearing the rumbling in my stomach. Being hungry is worse than freezing. It leaves you dizzy, weak, wanting to lie where you are because it's too hard to move.

That last morning I pulled myself up, thinking about meat. When I climbed out of the wagon, I saw Roanie in the meadow, his head up, his ears pricked so they almost touched, and hope flashed through me.

I reached for the rifle. If it was a deer or any animal big enough to get a sight on, could be I'd get lucky. "Steady," I said to myself. "Steady, and try not to miss."

Roanie snorted. Nickered deep down in his belly like a drum. And then I saw them. Horses. Four Indian riders coming single file through the trees.

I didn't know whether to be scared or get down on my knees and give thanks. They were people. They were real. I wasn't seeing a mirage or having a dream. It seemed I stood there an hour, not moving or making a sound because I couldn't. My throat felt swollen shut, so tight it made tears come.

There I stood, blubbering, my hands shaking so hard I dropped the rifle and didn't have the strength or the wit to bend and pick it up. I wrapped my arms around what was left of me and waited.

They rode right up to camp and stopped and stared at me. I must've looked a fright. Then, while one watched me, the others dismounted and nosed around the wagon, peeked into the house, all the time gabbling to themselves like a flock of hens. Then they came back to me.

One of them picked up the rifle, turned it over and over in his hands, then sighted along it—right past my head.

I found my voice. "Don't you dare shoot me!" I said. The thought of dying after what I'd been through must have given me courage.

He grinned, surprising me, but lowered the rifle and answered back. I didn't understand, but at least I wasn't looking down that long barrel.

"You have any food?" I asked.

He frowned and shook his head, but I figured he didn't know what I was saying, either. I rubbed my stomach, pretended I was eating, all the while looking him right in the face, into black eyes that told me nothing. "Damn it!" I said at last. "I'm hungry! Eat!" I saw spots dancing in front of me like a cloud of flies.

He must have told the others to check around again, and they did, bringing out the empty sacks of meal and, from the wagon, Pa's old jacket and pants—and the fiddle. One of them plucked the strings, and I saw they were busted. Well, for sure, everything was different now, broken and never to be fixed.

"Pa's gone!" I shouted. "I'm alone. Me!"—pointing at myself. "You take the clothes. Take the fiddle. I'll trade for food."

They got excited at that and walked around some more, examining the house, the little stove, my fry pan and kettle that hadn't been used in weeks. The friendly one pulled some dry moss out from the cracks in the walls, got wood from my pile, and somehow got a fire started.

Then I saw they had meat with them, fresh-killed. It was all I could do not to grab at it, my mouth was

27

watering so bad. I ate with my hands like they did, ate till I thought I'd get sick, my face and hands greasy and smeared with fat.

Whoever said Indians are devils didn't know *my* Indians. They saved me. We stayed in camp three days, and then, with a lot of signs and hand waving, they put me on Roanie, poor as he was, and I understood they were taking me away. I didn't care where—maybe to their village, to their women and children and warm teepees.

We rode out single file. When we got to the grove of trees, I pulled up and looked back—at the wagon, listing to one side, at the little house of logs and desperation, at the mountains poking holes in the sky.

There was a kind of sadness took me then, like I was leaving a place I'd come to know, saying good bye to home and to Pa and Jacky, wherever they were. No matter the hardship, I'd made out, and some part of me was back there, a ghost, a voice talking to itself, shattering the silence of the white winter snow.

We traveled for many days, slowly at first because of Roanie and me, and because of the mud that lay under the melting snow. The rivers were running high and dangerous, snaking between mountains and gorges, ice-cold and fast-moving. All along their banks, along the sides of the little creeks, frogs were croaking and singing, twanging like badly played guitars. I don't remember that I ever heard so many all at once, or that I was so glad to hear them. They were alive, and so was

I, and the men I traveled with treated me well.

They gave me a buffalo robe to sleep in, fed me what they ate themselves, laughed and chattered and kept my spirits up because I had no idea what was going to become of me.

Like everybody, I'd heard tales about captive white women, how they got raped, tattooed, turned into slaves, and starved, but nothing seemed as bad as what I'd already been through, and these men didn't do me any harm.

We got along with signs and noises. I talked American, and they talked in their own lingo, and after a while it didn't make any difference. We understood each other fine. The friendliest of them kept pointing west, across the mountains, and I figured he was trying to tell me that was where we were going.

As it turned out, they took me to Walla Walla, where I was a ten-day wonder—the girl who'd survived the winter by herself. The newspaper printed a story about me, and people came asking so many questions I couldn't follow them all and making me wish, sometimes, to be back in the quiet.

That's a funny thing, how I got used to silence, and how the bustle and noise of the town screeched in my ears till they hurt. But it looks like I'll stay right here. I've got no place else to go, no one to run to. I'm still alone, even with people all around.

The sun came up red that April morning. Its long rays touched the faces of the family around the breakfast table with the color of blood.

And there will be more blood, Livvy thought. *How would it end?* It seemed that every time she found security and peace, they were taken away, leaving her to begin again as a different Livvy, a woman she didn't know or understand.

She had been six when the Quahadi Comanches killed her parents and carried her off, and twelve when she was recaptured and adopted by Nolan and Willa Hightower. Nolan had been her father's friend back in Tennessee, and he and Willa had taken her in as soon as they heard she'd been found.

Livvy's adjustment back into the white world hadn't been easy. She had come to love her Comanche foster parents, and she missed them and the freedom of life on the plains. But from the first there had been Sim, the youngest, the hottest tempered of the Hightower sons. He'd teased her without mercy, wrestled with her and, to his shame, lost, and finally, to the astonishment of them both, their childhood wrangling had turned to love. They had been married four months.

Four months! she thought. She'd hoped for a lifetime surrounded by the warmth of husband and family. As always, circumstances were forcing her into a role she didn't want and had never imagined. She swallowed hard and listened to Nolan Hightower whose presence dominated the room.

Nolan had come to Texas after the war and had built a Texas cattle empire out of guts, common sense, and hard work, only to have it threatened by lawlessness and a feud that had its roots in the mountains of Tennessee.

Nobody rightly remembered how the bad blood between Hightowers and Cordells began, but in the past year the old hatred between the two families had erupted into violence.

The trouble started when Nolan caught Buzz and Roy Cordell, branding Hightower calves. Even the sheriff, Sam Brant, who was in the Cordell's pocket, couldn't keep Buzz and Roy from going over the road to Huntsville, but they'd been let out on bail. Like all the Cordells, they had come back looking for revenge, even if it killed them. It had, but not before Seth, the oldest Hightower son, lay buried, and Sim's prize mares had been destroyed.

Sim found the mares in the corral screaming, their tongues cut out, their aborted foals trampled in the dust. Heartsick, he and Nolan led the mutilated animals out on the range and shot them. They rode home in silence, each struggling with anger and revulsion.

When he could trust his voice, Sim said: "Let's go after 'em, Pa. They left a trail the schoolmarm could follow."

Nolan shook his head. "Not this time. We'll let the

law take its course. We can't go on feudin' forever."

"Damn it, Pa! They've got to be stopped. Cuttin' those mares. . . ."

"Those mares aren't worth losing another son," Nolan interrupted him. "Losing Seth nearly killed your ma."

It had nearly killed Sim, too. He'd been the one who found his brother after the Cordells caught Seth short, ran him into a barn, and set fire to it. When Seth came out, they shot him down, then swore they'd been nowhere near the place and had witnesses to back them.

"It was. . . . Cordells," Seth had whispered through burned lips. "Tell Ma I love her." Then he was gone.

The memory was fresh in Sim's mind, fueling his anger, but he followed his father back to the corral and unsaddled. He had his own plan, and it didn't include Nolan. As long as he lived, he'd remember Seth's face and the terror in the mares' eyes. As long as he lived, the Cordells were in danger. He wiped down his horse, threw out some hay, then went to the house and found Livvy.

"What're you aimin' to do?" she asked, sickened by the tragedy and knowing Sim only too well.

"You're going to get me a horse and leave it and my Winchester in the timber down by the creek. I'm cuttin' out after supper, and I won't be back till I've done what needs doin'."

"You want a back-up?" At times like this, it was still hard being white. All her instincts urged her to fight alongside her man.

32

"This is my business." Sim kissed her to take the sting out of his words. *"I'll be fine. You just do what I said, and don't tell Pa."*

He'd been right about the trail the killers had left—like they were begging to be tracked and were waiting somewhere in ambush. Riding cautiously, it was after midnight when Sim reached the shack. Two horses dozed in a brush corral, and a wisp of smoke came from the rude chimney, although no light showed through the window. Sim settled himself against a tree, the Winchester in his lap, and took up his vigil. Morning would come soon enough.

The sun had just topped the edge of the plain when Buzz and Roy stumbled out. They never saw who shot them, never saw Sim mount his big roan and head for home, but two of Cameron Cordell's hands who were driving a small bunch of horses did see, and wasted no time reporting the killing.

Sam Brant showed up with a warrant hours later, but Sim was long gone. He spent a week, hiding out in the brush, but finally decided he'd had enough. He missed his bride, and he wasn't afraid of the sheriff or of old man Cordell, either.

Livvy heard the crack of a pebble against her window. A moment later she pushed it open and called out: *"That you?"*

"None other." Sim crawled through and took her in his arms. *"I took a bath in the creek,"* he said with a

grin. *"Left my horse there in case I have to cut out, but, dammit, I missed you bad."*

"Me, too," she said, her face buried in his chest. God, she'd been lonely! And afraid—more for him than for herself. Without Sim she felt cut in half, purposeless, like dry rain that fell without touching the ground. *"When you leave, I'm coming along,"* she told him. *"And don't say I can't."*

"No more talk." He picked her up and carried her to the bed. *"Talk's for daylight."*

Now they were talking, or rather Nolan was, and he was laying down the law, his eyes icy blue and stern.

"I don't blame you a damn' bit for what you done," he told Sim. "But the fact is, you're wanted for murder, and you're going to have to slope. I wish things were different, but they aren't. We're stuck with Brant, swilling at the same trough with the Cordells and their rustler crowd, and, if he don't get you, he'll call in the Rangers."

Sim's eyes were replicas of his father's. "I oughta go after the whole bunch. String Brant up along with the rest."

Nolan slapped his hand on the table, rattling the dishes, but his expression didn't change. "I'm tellin' you that you're headin' north and catch up with Bob and the crew. They can use another hand pushin' them mares. Once you get across the Red, Texas law can't touch you. Leastways, not legal."

What Sim thought about running showed on his face,

and Livvy read it. So did Willa, who reached out and took her son's hand. Sim had always been her favorite—the wild one that needed tending to.

"We don't want to see you hung," she said softly. "And I don't want another grave alongside Seth's. Do what your pa wants, and, if everything works out, we'll all get to Nebraska without more killing."

Willa bit her lip to keep it from trembling. So many deaths, and for what? The quicker they got out of Texas, the better she'd feel.

Sim sighed, knowing he was beat but hating the fact that he'd be leaving Livvy behind. "Are you with them on this, too?" he asked.

Three days before, the Hightower horses, three hundred head of Steel-Dust/Shiloh mares, some with colts at their sides, had left for the new ranch in Nebraska. If Sim's future was to be there, she'd be alongside him. She reckoned she could be happy anywhere as long as she was with him, but the thought of staying behind lay in her belly like a stone. "I'm going with you," she said, the glance she shot at Nolan defiant.

Nolan nodded. "I figured you'd say that, but the trail's no place for a woman." At the look on her face, he added: "I can't forbid you, but me and your ma hope you'll stay here till Sim sends word."

He looked at Sim, and Livvy's heart sank. Of course, Sim would agree with his father. He always had. But she wanted, needed, to be riding at his side.

"Pa's right," Sim said finally. "Drivin' horses ain't like pushin' cows. And every rustler and brave off the reservation is goin' to be lookin' to steal themselves a bunch of horses."

Livvy snorted. If they ran into Comanches, she'd be a help. She spoke their language and had been raised with Quanah Parker. Still, it was obvious the men had made up their minds, so she managed to conceal what she was thinking and give them a sorrowful smile. *Just you wait!* she thought. *Just you wait!*

It was easy to say a tearful good bye. Who knew what might happen to Sim before he caught up with his brother? Who knew what or where the Cordells would strike next? "Take care," she whispered, her arms around his neck. "Please, honey." Then she turned and ran, not wanting to watch him out of sight. Besides, she had a plan to put in motion.

Two nights later, she was ready. Her things lay spread out on her bed, ready for a final check, and Eufemio, the Mexican hand who thought he was her second father, had her horse saddled and tied down at the creek bottom.

With her, she would carry her slicker, two blankets and a tarp, a picket pin and rope, a full canteen, and, if she knew Eufemio and his woman, María, some tamales wrapped in the newspaper she could use to start fires, a little coffee pot, coffee, sugar, beans, tortillas, jerky, a Bowie knife, her lariat, and a pair of hobbles. It would make a bundle behind her saddle, but she knew how to travel the prairies.

She also had Sim's Colt .45 in its worn leather holster,

and a full cartridge belt, plus her own Winchester '73, fully loaded. In her war bag she carried coat and gloves, extra shirt, socks, and underwear, soap, a comb, her toothbrush, and a pair of field glasses. She'd rifled Willa's old trunk for a pair of outgrown boy's trousers, the only garment fit to ride in, and had added a flannel shirt and a vest with pockets for extra ammunition and a dozen matches stored in two tightly sealed cartridge cases.

Almost ready! By the time her absence was discovered, it would be morning, hopefully too late for Nolan to come after her. She jumped when the knock came on her door.

"Who is it?" she asked, trying to shove her things under the bed.

"Ma."

It was futile to hide her intent, especially since she hadn't time to put on a dress. She'd simply have to convince Willa that she was going whether or not she had the blessing of her parents.

Willa came in, took one look, and grinned. "I knew it!" she said, grinning harder. "I reckon that noise was you sweeping your getaway outfit under the bed."

"How'd you know?"

"Any woman worth having could've figured it out. I'd come along except Nolan would run us both down." She opened her arms and hugged her daughter tightly.

"I thought you'd be mad," Livvy whispered.

"Mad!" Willa snorted. "We're women. We know what it's like always being left behind to worry, always being told we're helpless and need lookin' after. You love Sim. Your place is with him. I come to help you get your things together, and I brought you something I figure you might need."

She pulled a small pistol from her apron pocket. "It's a double barrel Derringer. Got a clip to fasten it to the top of your boot. If you keep your pants down over, nobody knows you've got it."

Livvy took the deadly little pistol and hefted it. "Where'd you get this?"

"Had an uncle who was a gambler. Last time he got it out a little too late. They sent his things to me as his only relative." She laughed. "If you need it, don't wait like he did. It's a Forty-One. Makes quite a hole. Here's some extra rounds."

Willa was tough and a realist. If the girl was set on going, the better armed she was, the better her chances. Between that and her life with the Comanches, she'd make out. "Come on," she said. "I'll walk you down to the creek."

"You figured that out, too," Livvy said, lifting her war bag. "Is there anything that goes on around here you don't know?"

"Not much. Give me the bedroll and the tarp. We'll go out the back way just so your pa won't hear. First, give me a kiss for luck."

Belle, Livvy's mare, nickered softly as they approached. She was big for a mare, sixteen hands, a red bay, intelligent and tireless. As Livvy fastened the Winchester scabbard and tied down her bundles, Belle danced, sensing that their trip would be a long one, and she was eager to be gone.

"Don't worry, Ma. I'll be fine. So will Sim." Livvy looked down on Willa from the saddle and heard the concern in her mother's voice.

"Oh, I know. If I didn't, I'd hog-tie you and keep you here. Just be careful. I'll be prayin' for you day and night. Now git before your pa turns over and finds I'm out of bed!" She patted Livvy's leg, then slapped the mare on her haunch, and stepped back into the shadows.

Livvy put several miles between her and the house before she bedded down for the night. She made a dry camp and didn't light a fire. A few swallows of cold water took the place of coffee before she pulled off her boots and vest, and turned in, using her rolled slicker for a pillow and shoving her six-shooter under it. Belle was grazing close by, and the scent of crushed grass filled the night with sweetness.

Before she fell asleep, Livvy looked up at the sky and wondered what the future had in store. Even Nolan and Willa were planning to pull out of Texas and away from the rustling and the feud that had already cost them one son and might take Sim, especially if he took it in his head to return.

She thought of the mares with their tongues cut out, and how she'd been the one to send Sim after the scum that had done it. In that way, they were alike, easily angered at useless killing, easily brought to wildness.

An eye for an eye, she thought bitterly, and none of it

would stop as long as they hung on in Texas. Even Nolan, as tough as he was, admitted that. The killings, the violence would continue until all the Hightowers, or all their enemies, were rubbed out.

Livvy awoke at the first faint light in the east. Belle was asleep nearby but, when Livvy stirred, woke and nickered softly, probably thinking about oats.

"Sorry, old girl. There wasn't room for them on top of the rest," she said as she pulled on her boots. "But I bet you won't turn down a tortilla."

The mare nickered again and watched as Livvy built a small fire and brewed coffee, waiting her turn for the hand-out she knew from experience was coming.

As a small white girl struggling with the loss of a second and much loved set of parents and attempting to fit in to a life she'd almost forgotten, Livvy's best friend, next to Sim, had been the little bay filly, a gift from Nolan who figured his new daughter needed something of her own to love, and that time would take care of the rest. He'd been right.

Livvy had talked in two languages, and the filly had listened. Now it seemed like Belle could read her mind, her every move, and rarely argued the point.

"We know where we're headed," she said as she saddled up. "We'll just keep after those mares, and keep our eyes open, too. Can't ever tell when those damned Cordells or some of their friends might be hiding in the brush." Even as she spoke, she felt as if something, somewhere was wrong.

The faint smell of wood smoke was her first inkling

40

that her instincts had been right. Rifle out, she moved upwind, listening with her head cocked to one side. From somewhere came the bawling of a calf, and she rode toward the sound, realizing that someone had a branding fire going.

It wasn't branding time, and this part of the High-tower range, far from headquarters, had been rustled over, time and again. Well, not today. Not if she could help it. She slipped into a clump of mesquite and dis-mounted, moving as silently as any Comanche toward the scent of smoke, the bawling of the calf.

Below her, in a small clearing, a man was heating a running iron, the calf tied and ready to brand. Its mother had been heeled and thrown some distance away, held there by a second rider who dragged her every time she tried to struggle up to go to her calf.

How dare they? How dare these rustlers come in and help themselves to Hightower property? And in such a cruel way? At roundup time the calves were separated from their mothers and branded in small corrals while the mothers paced outside.

Livvy set her jaw and struggled to control her anger. No sense going in with emotion ruling her, but she'd be damned if they'd abuse or steal any more Hightower property!

She drew a careful bead on the rustler by the fire and shot him in the leg, but she hadn't given a thought to the second rider, who dropped his rope and headed toward her.

"You thievin' son-of-a-bitch!" she yelled, and

dropped him in the dirt.

Once back in the saddle, she remembered the calf, tied fast and certain to die of starvation or thirst unless she freed it. The first downed man was still conscious, thrashing around on the ground beside the fire. Dismounting, she covered her face with her bandanna and walked toward the calf.

The man on the ground was clutching his leg and blubbering. "You . . . you . . . ," he got out, then stopped when she pulled her pistol.

"Cut him loose," she ordered, recognizing one of the Cordell boys whose name she didn't know.

"I can't! It hurts like hell."

"You heard me. Or do you want another round? Take you out of your misery."

Groaning, he swiveled and pulled the piggin' strings loose. "We'll get you for this," he muttered between clenched teeth.

"You'll have to find me first."

At the sound of an approaching rider, she ran for Belle and headed for the brush at a lope.

"What in hell's goin' on here?"

With a shock, Livvy recognized the roar that was old man Cameron Cordell's usual speaking voice.

Now she was in for it. Now he'd follow and try to gun her down, the latest victim of the senseless feud, unless she could lose him, hide her tracks in the creek, and hope he couldn't pick them up again when she hit the prairie. She was a killer, a renegade as much as Sim, and no two ways about it. Calling on all the skills learned from her Indian family, she put Belle into the water and headed northwest.

Cameron Cordell brought a wagon to put his "damn' fool son," Wat, in, along with the body of Dave, his favorite.

Wat was one of his sons by his first wife. Cameron had five boys before he realized he'd married bad blood. When that first wife died, he hadn't missed her a minute. In two months he found a young replacement, a woman who was a hard worker and who loved him and showed it. That had been twenty years before, and she'd given him two more sons and three girls, whom he thought of as "the good seed."

Only now Dave was dead, and he had no idea who to blame except himself. He had tried to keep Dave away from the others, but, hell, he couldn't keep an eye on him forever. Boys had to grow up sometime. Now Dave was lying twisted and still in the wagon bed next to Wat who had finally passed out from shock.

"Serve you right if you die, too. I wish you'd died, instead," Cameron said over his shoulder. He had a notion to shoot Wat himself. Like Nolan Hightower, he was getting tired of the killings year after year, most of which involved his "bad seed."

Horseman that he was, Cameron had gagged at the cruelty involved in cutting Sim's prize mares. He had never really blamed Sim for killing Buzz and Roy. It was the kind of thing that he might have shot them for himself. In any case, the score was now three to one, might be four if Wat died from loss of blood.

Who was next? Before Wat passed out, he had described the rider who'd shot him. "A little redhead. Not much more'n a kid." If it wasn't a Hightower or any of their men, who could it have been? Maybe a stranger, but what was his motive? The fact of a loose cannon roaming the territory was disturbing. The Cordells had enough trouble as it was. Cameron decided to follow the killer's tracks back where they came from before looking for those leaving the scene of the shooting. The burying of Dave would be up to his wife, who'd mourn her first-born but understand that her husband had no time to waste.

He closed his eyes, shutting off tears. When he opened them again, his face was set in stone.

Livvy rode ten miles before she pulled Belle up out of the creek onto the prairie. There, like a Comanche, she rode in long, curving paths, watching her back trail for anyone following her seemingly idle tracks.

It took two days before she spotted the rider who was just far enough behind that she couldn't make out either him or his horse, but she would have bet that somehow Cameron Cordell had picked up her sign. If he caught up with her, he would show no mercy. After all, she was a Hightower now, and a killer.

She clucked to Belle. "It's up to us," she told the mare. "We've got to ditch him and do it quick."

Belle moved into her ground-covering trot, a gait she could hold for hours without tiring, and, when they hit another creek, they went into it, changing directions, and, with luck, confusing the rider behind.

When Cameron had left the scene of the shooting, he had followed the killer's tracks back to where Livvy had camped, then to the creek at the Hightower house, a puzzle for sure.

"Who in hell do they have workin' for them with red hair?" he muttered to himself. Maybe they'd hired new. Maybe a range detective who did what he was paid for and sloped, but that didn't figure. The Hightowers did their own killing.

Still, if it came to it, he was going to have it out with Nolan, or be damned. It was time to fetch the killing to a close. Past time. At the thought of Dave, he spurred his horse and went in search of the unknown killer.

When he finally found the way Livvy had taken out of the second creek, he was at least a day behind her, but she wasn't taking anything for granted. If it came to it, she'd dry-gulch her pursuer. She had killed once; she guessed she could do it a second time. Nonetheless, she heaved a sigh of relief when, after a week, she caught up with the wagon and herd just south of Doan's Crossing.

"Somebody comin'. Lickety-split." Solly, the chuck wagon cook, squinted into the distance.

Sim jumped to his feet. "Now what?"

Solly, who had eyes like a hawk, said: "It's Miz Livvy. Darned if it ain't!"

Sim felt his heart sink. The only reason Livvy could

45

be here was trouble. He grabbed the reins of the closest horse and rode out to meet her.

"It's all right!" she called, reading his concern from a distance. "It's just me . . . come to lend a hand."

She was smiling, half relieved, half joyful, and covered with dust, but, to Sim, she looked beautiful just the way she was—wild, determined, passionate. Back at the wagon, in spite of Solly, he kissed her, hard, knocking her hat to the ground so her hair tumbled to her shoulders.

"God, it's good to see you!" he said when he caught his breath. Then: "Does Pa know?"

"Nope!" She smiled harder, her eyes twinkling. "Well, by now he does, but Ma knew from the start. She helped me."

"She would." He hesitated a minute, sensing a difference in her but unable to pinpoint exactly what it was. "You're sure everything's all right?"

"Mostly." She walked to the shade of the wagon. "Can I have some water?" she asked Solly. "My canteen's nearly empty."

"Yes'm, you can. You sit right down, and we'll get the questions asked when you're done. And Mister Sim, mebbe you should unsaddle old Belle. She looks like she wants to roll."

That was Solly, always kind, always filled with common sense. She took the cup he offered and drank, letting the water wash away the dust in her throat, the miles she had covered. After a minute, she wiped her face on her sleeve.

46

"You'd better know," she began. "I killed one of Cordell's boys back there, and the old man's on my trail."

Sim turned, stunned by her normal tone. "How?"

She set the cup down and laughed. "I shot him. There were two of them, branding one of our calves. I shot one in the leg, and, when the other came after me, I shot him, too. Then I cut out of there fast. Cameron Cordell heard the shots and came runnin', but I ditched him. He'll be comin', though. I guess, now, we're both in trouble."

"You're sure the one you cut down's dead?"

"I don't miss."

Unexpectedly Sim laughed. "That's one less of them."

"You're not mad?"

"I'm damn' proud, if you want to know. Bob may be a little riled when he hears, but he's that way all the time anyhow. All he wants is to get to Nebraska without trouble. Looks like he won't, not if that old buzzard's on your trail. But at least you're here, not out on your own. We'll give him what he deserves if he tries anything."

"We will at that." Solly was washing the dinner plates in his big, tin tub. "Now you better eat something, Miz Livvy. You're gonna need your strength."

She was hungry. Cold camps and stale tortillas were hardly enough to fuel what she'd been through. Still, there had been times with the Comanches when nobody had eaten for days, and there had been no complaints, only the will to endure. She took the plate of Solly's fragrant stew, her mouth watering. "I'm so hungry I could eat a whole side of beef," she said, and never noticed the look of admiration that passed between her husband and the cook. If she had, she would have wondered what she'd done to deserve it.

From his hidden camp in the brush, Cameron trained his field glasses on the Hightower outfit. He recognized Sim, Bob, and Solly, and the three Mexicans circling the herd, but there wasn't a redhead in sight.

Although he'd lost Livvy's trail, the general direction had been toward Doan's Crossing, so he'd made a run for it and arrived shortly after she did. He bought a few supplies from Doan's store, asked no questions, and headed for a place where he could see but not be seen. Now he moved closer to the camp, sat down, and steadied his glasses. After what seemed hours, he saw Livvy ride in. His jaw dropped at the sight of her in Sim's arms, her red hair spilling down to her shoulders.

"It can't be the gal," he muttered, then thought back. She'd been with the Comanches, and she rode and covered her trail like one. It could have been she who'd shot his boys. Hell, she was a squaw, regardless of the color of her skin, her Hightower connections. He'd killed a few Indian women when he was in the cavalry for no reason except they'd been there. This time, he figured, he had a damned good reason, *if* he could be sure.

"One of these days, missy, I'll pick up your tracks,"

he said. "Count on it, if I have to follow you to hell and back."

He swung his glasses toward the south as a group of riders appeared and headed in his direction. Stiffly, cursing his bad knee, he got up and moved farther into the brush.

Sim was the first to see the riders. He'd been as alert as a hunted fox since Livvy had come in. Judging from the past, the Cordells were capable of mass murder, and neither he nor Bob were about to take chances.

"Trouble coming for real," he said, recognizing Sam Brant, Ike and Tom, two of Cameron's bad seeds, Cap Arrington, the Texas Ranger, and another Ranger.

"Spread out and let me do the talking," Bob said, his face grim. "Be ready for anything."

Arrington read the move and wasn't about to predict what would happen if Ike and Tom and the rube sheriff took it in their heads to start trouble. "If there's gonna be any shooting, let me start it," he told them. "You all sit tight. I'm running this show, so mind me."

As he approached the camp, he said to Bob: "Howdy. Cap Arrington of the Rangers."

Bob looked him over. "I reckon I've heard of you," he said, then grinned. "I reckon everybody's heard of you. What can we do for you?"

"I've got a warrant here for Sim Hightower. Where might I find him?"

"He's my brother. What's he wanted for?"

Ike Cordell butted in with a snarl. "For murdering my

49

brothers. And that's him . . . right over there."

"Shut up," Arrington growled. To Bob he said: "Is he here?"

"He was the last time I looked. But he ain't the kind to kill anybody without reason. I admit he killed a couple of skunks that cut the tongues out of two of our mares."

Arrington's eyes narrowed. "What for?"

Bob told him, adding: "Butchering two good horses ain't exactly fighting square."

"That's a damn' lie!" Ike yelled. "You tell him, Brant."

The sheriff cleared his throat, keeping quiet, but Arrington moved his horse next to Ike's and, without warning, knocked Ike off it with the barrel of his six-shooter. "I told you to shut up, and I meant it," he said, then turned back to Bob.

"I reckon your daddy might be the Colonel High-tower that rode with Forrest. Is that so?"

Sensing that the Ranger was up to something, Bob nodded. "That's him."

Arrington looked at Tom Cordell. "I heard your daddy was a state policeman before we got rid of those damnyankee carpetbaggers a couple years ago. That so?"

"He was a good lawman," Tom muttered.

The Ranger grunted and cast an eye on the Hightower crew. "I reckon y'all are aimin' to shoot it out with me and the boys if I try to take your brother in."

Bob shook his head. "No, we ain't. I'd trust him with

you, but, if he gets back home, that sheriff you got with you has a habit of looking the other way while Cordells shoot Hightowers. And cut their horses," he added.

Ike moaned, and Arrington looked down at him with disgust. "You and Tom get the hell back to the store and take this one with you," he said to Brant. "I'll bring your man over in a bit."

Once they were on their way, he asked: "Mind if we get down and rest our hindquarters?"

In answer Bob said: "We've got coffee, and Solly can heat up some of his stew."

"Sounds good." The two Rangers stepped down, leaving their horses on dropped reins.

Livvy was thinking that Sim had a chance with this man, but, no matter what, if they took him in, she was going along. She slipped her arm under his and stood by him, fighting the fear and pain in her heart.

Arrington wasn't one to beat around the bush. He called Bob aside and said in a low voice: "I was with Mosby during the war. Guerillas didn't operate according to the book, and I reckon I haven't changed much. We didn't have the authority to give paroles, but, when a good man came along, we gave one. The rest we sorta lost in the woods."

Bob nodded and studied the Ranger's serious face. It seemed like they might get Sim out of this yet, but he decided to stay quiet and see what came next.

Arrington looked away. "I got my reputation to think about, of course, and I've had some hard things said about me in my time, but I can take it. What you said . . . about those horses and all. Was that the truth?"

Bob nodded again. "A hell of a way to get revenge."

"Cowardly," Arrington said, then allowed himself a smile. "I'd like you to do me a favor. Me and Mort are gonna eat our dinner, facing west." He was enjoying himself like a good storyteller, with Bob hanging on every word. "Now, what I'd like you to do is have your brother saddle up, ride north, and get the hell across the Red as fast as his horse can go. We don't have any jurisdiction over there, and I'll see that the hayseed sheriff and those two sons-of-bitches with him don't follow right away."

Bob let out the breath he'd been holding. "I don't know how to thank you."

"No thanks needed. Just give your daddy my respects when you see him next." He walked back to the wagon and took the plate Solly handed him, then sat down with his back against the wheel, staring at the sun that was just beginning to set.

Through his field glasses, Cameron saw Sim cut and run for the Red, with Livvy only minutes behind him. Stunned, he realized that Arrington had let the kid go, while Ike, Tom, and Brant, like the idiots they were, cooled their heels at Doan's. But not for long. This was his chance to even the score with Sim, and, if the gal was the same red-headed kid who'd killed Dave and led him a chase across half of Texas, he'd find out and get her, too.

Quickly he broke camp and headed for the store. The sooner he collected his sons and hit the trail, the better. As for Brant—Cameron snorted—he could go home and stay put. At least there he was useful. Where the three Cordells were headed, he'd simply be a damned nuisance.

Livvy caught the scent of the river before she reached it—the scent of a thousand miles of water, red as the earth through which it ran and always unreliable. She pulled up on the bluff, and memories that had been submerged surfaced slowly, tugging at her heart. It was almost as if she could see them, the *Nermernuh*, The People, coming toward her, men, women, children, mounted on their ponies, and behind them a herd of a thousand more, the hoof beats loud, the voices of the children rising above all—a music of drums and fluting laughter, a trick of the mind, a dream recalled.

In the long shadows of evening, she saw her adopted family—Stone Ear and Turns Around, and her friend, Quanah Parker, whose mother had been white. He had been the first to show her kindness, letting her ride his warbonnet paint horse, teasing her about the color of her hair that, even unwashed, shone like a beacon.

Where were they now? she wondered. Perhaps dead, hunted down without mercy, or forced onto the reservation to starve and cling to the old ways that were vanishing, and with them the taste of long winds, the sweetness of rain.

She was here, lone rider at a boundary. On one side was Texas, on the other, Indian Territory, both of which she could call home.

Sim had made it across. Her horse, fresh from the remuda, snorted, danced sideways, asked for its head. She loosened the reins and let him carry her down the bank and into the river.

In the long twilight, she and Sim put ten miles between themselves and the crossing. "Just in case Cameron's around and takes it in his head to come after us." Sim spoke from long experience. "With scum like them, you can't be sure of anything," he added.

"That's why I changed horses. If he was tracking Belle, she's back with the herd. Let him figure that out. Besides, she needed a rest." *So do I*, she thought, but didn't say.

"Think we'll ever get one?" Sim asked, reading her mind.

She laughed. "Not till we're old. Maybe not then."

He hoped they lived to be old, to see their sons and daughters, their children's children, and the Hightower empire secure. That was his father's dream, and his own, but he wasn't sure the paradise they visualized existed anywhere.

Slowing his horse, he said: "Let's find a place to camp before dark."

Livvy looked around. They were in a country of ridges, cañons, long plains—Comanche country, well remembered. "Down there." She pointed to a defile winding between hills. "There's water and grass."

"How do you know?"

She smiled. "This is my place, remember?"

Although the Quahadis lived far to the west, they had often come here after a buffalo, had wandered as the hunt led them, owners of the earth. Young as she had been, she still knew where to find water, food, shelter. Hunters and hunted never forgot the land that gave them life.

"What was it like?" Sim wanted to know. They were sitting beside a small fire that gave off little light. "With the Comanches, I mean."

He'd never asked before, probably afraid of what she'd say. She stretched out beside him. "Different."

"How?"

Could she say it was holy in spite of hunger, filth, constant struggle? Could she say to this man, her husband whom she loved, that there had been a joy, a feeling that the whole earth was hers?

"No matter what anybody thinks now, it was beautiful. Hard . . . but beautiful."

He saw her face illuminated by the fire, saw the night sky, star-dazzled, heard the breath of horses, the sizzle of damp logs. A *Tejano* born and bred, a lover of open space and emptiness, he had the ability to hear what wasn't audible.

"Reckon it was at that," he said. "Just like now."

"Yes," she agreed. "Just like now."

Then they were silent, both listening to the murmuring of earth.

"The old man didn't waste any time." Sim was looking south through the glasses. "He must've been right on your heels, because it looks like he picked up Ike and Tom, too."

"Is it them?"

"See for yourself."

She picked up three riders so far off they were blurs on the edge of the prairie but moving toward them at a steady jog. "I should've got him when I had the chance," she muttered, shoving the glasses into her saddlebag.

This was how the Comanches must feel—harried by Mackenzie and his soldiers, never knowing when confrontation would come, only that it was inevitable. She fought down anger—for herself and The People whom she had once known and loved. "You want to circle around and dry-gulch them?" she asked.

On his own, Sim would have done just that, but his concern was for her. "Let's join up with the rest. Safer that way."

"But they'll still be out there."

"Sure, but, when it comes to a showdown, there'll be seven of us and three of them. I like those odds."

He was right, of course, but she was stubborn, and she was counting on the wildness that, in him, was never far below the surface. "All right, but let's lead them a little chase first. Slow them down."

Without waiting for his answer, she kicked her horse into a lope. Giving a fair imitation of the rebel yell, Sim followed.

Responsibility sat heavily on Bob's shoulders, and his face showed the strain as Livvy and Sim rode into camp. " 'Bout time you got here," he said. "I was figurin' to send out a search party. Everything all right?"

Sim wiped his face on his sleeve. "Just ridin' in circles, Brother. Hoping to confuse the enemy."

Bob muttered a curse. "Sorry, Livvy. Arrington said he'd try to hold those bastards up."

She shrugged. "Obviously he didn't. Or couldn't. And obviously the old man's with them. So we decided to make us a little hard to follow."

"What d'you think they'll try?" Bob asked Sim.

"Maybe pick us off one at a time. At least me and Livvy, seein' as we're the ones they're after. But we can't put anything past them. Hell, they might sneak up and bump all of us . . . take the hosses and line their damned pockets."

Bob paced in a circle, kicking a stone ahead of him. "Let 'em try. They'll play hell sneakin' up on Julio. He sees in the dark."

"Miz Livvy's gonna sleep in the wagon." Solly was scowling. Any threat to a Hightower was a threat to him personally. "She'll sleep in the wagon, and I'll be right here with the shotgun. No Cordell's gonna come sneakin' past me."

At the thought of sleep, Livvy stifled a yawn. She hadn't realized how tired she was, unusually so for her, although the past ten days had been a physical and mental strain. "If nobody minds, I'll turn in," she said.

"You can fill me in on your plans in the morning."

"I can tell you right now." Bob kicked the stone into the fire and watched as it scattered ashes. "First light . . . we're headin' out. The more distance we put between us and them the better I'll like it. We haven't hit bad weather yet, but we might. And we haven't seen any Injuns, but they're out there. The Cordells are just one more problem I don't need."

"And it's my fault, I guess." Sim could feel his anger mounting. As always, his older brother managed to make him feel guilty.

Solly stepped between the two. "It's nobody's fault, 'cept those no-good skunks that don't know no better. What we don't need is you two fightin' like you did when you was babies . . . and got a whuppin' from Mister Nolan to boot."

"Solly's right. No matter what, we're all in this together. Getting mad won't solve anything."

Livvy yawned again, then smiled at the two brothers. "Coming, Sim?"

Hell, they were both right, and he knew it. He was partly at fault, no matter who said what, and he'd better just shut up. "In a minute," he said. "Get to sleep."

But as tired as Livvy was, sleep didn't come. For a long time she lay awake watching the shadows of the fire on the canvas wagon walls, listening to the night sounds that intensified the prairie silence.

Earth went on regardless of feuds and men. It existed whether or not it was fought over, plowed under, sectioned off. The rivers ran, the wind blew, and there was comfort in that, in the recognition of another, more powerful order.

When Sim finally came in and lay beside her, she curled against his warmth and closed her eyes.

Before dawn the wind picked up, slowly at first, small gusts separated by calm, and then harder, steadier, in bursts of strength. The mares were skittish, the urge to move away from the weather making them hard to hold.

Solly poured a bucket of water over the fire and scattered the ashes. "No sense burnin' down the prairie," he said to Livvy. "Once you see a fire out here, you don't want to see another. Supper's gonna be cold beans and bread unless I miss my guess."

"I guess we'll live," she said, although the way she felt, she wouldn't bet on it. She grabbed Belle's reins as the mare stuck her nose inside the wagon. "You quit!"

Solly grinned. "That's the beggin'est hoss I ever saw. Give her a chunk of that bread, and eat some yourself. You didn't eat enough to keep a bird alive. Mebbe you oughta ride with me today." He hoped she would. There were times when, with only the mules for company, the miles seemed longer than they were.

"I'd better go out with the boys. They'll need all the help they can get." Livvy offered the bread, and Belle took it carefully.

"Those hosses gonna want to run with the wind up their tails," Solly agreed. "You go on. I'll get where we're goin'."

59

Solly's prediction was a true one. The mares, like all horses, allied themselves with the wind, refusing to settle, attempting to break away and run on their own. In the lead, Bob set a fast pace, but the other riders were kept busy running down strays and pushing them back to the herd.

Wind was the enemy, Livvy thought, wind and the dust that rose and stung her eyes, choked her, and made her want to scream in frustration.

A brown mare broke and ran, tail high, and Livvy went after her, cussing under her breath when the mare stepped in a hole and fell, tumbling end over end, and then struggled to stand on three legs. Sickened, she pulled up and jumped off Belle, trying not to frighten the already crazed mare.

"Easy, girl," she crooned, but the wind carried her words away.

Sim came up beside her, his face set. "Broken?"

She nodded. "Damn it! It's such a waste! All of it. This shouldn't have happened. She's such a beauty."

He handed her his reins and pulled his .45. "I'll take care of it."

She turned and led the horses away, shoulders hunched, waiting for the sound of the shot. *One less*, she thought. *How many more will never make it?*

The report was loud and final, and she blinked back tears. The killing of an animal was almost worse than the killing of a human, but why that was so was a riddle she was too tired to solve.

"It hurts," she said as they rode away from the

pathetic heap on the ground. "I hate just leaving her here."

"At least she's not alone." Sim nodded at the piles of buffalo bones that littered the ground. "The buffalo hunters've been busy."

She remembered the thrill of the hunts, the sight of thousands of buffalo stampeding across the prairie, and the excitement of the Comanche women and children as they skinned and gutted the dead beasts, fighting over liver and intestines. Not a pretty sight in the eyes of whites, but neither were the bones of the animals that had been shot only for their hides, the bodies left to rot, fit only as food for predators.

She didn't answer, simply turned and headed back toward the herd. What was done was done. In a few more years all the buffalo would be gone, replaced by white men's cattle. In a few more years the Comanches, too, would disappear, remembered only in books and stories told around campfires and dinner tables, and she was glad she wasn't there to witness the end of a people.

The wind blew for two days. On the evening of the second day it suddenly stopped, replaced by dark clouds on the western horizon.

Bob shook his head. "I was wonderin' when we'd hit bad weather. Looks like tomorrow we're gonna get a little wet. It'll make crossin' the Canadian that much harder."

"Long as it don't blow." Solly had the stew pot bubbling over the first fire he'd made since the wind started. "I can stand near' anything but that wind."

Livvy still had grit squeaking between her teeth, in spite of the bandanna she'd kept over her nose and mouth, but she knew only too well what a real storm on the plains could mean. "Careful what you wish for, Solly," she said. "You might get it in spades."

He spat into the fire. "Then I wish them Cordells would get themselves lost. They was followin' me most of the afternoon. Just far enough back so I couldn't get a shot at 'em."

"Waitin' their chance, like the coyotes, they are," Sim said. "I might just circle around behind and catch 'em unawares."

"No you won't," Livvy and Bob said simultaneously.

"Just an idea."

"And a bad one. I'm gonna need all the help I can get when that storm hits. And it will."

He was right. Livvy felt the change of weather down her spine. It was going to storm, and storm hard, probably by morning. The mares knew it, too. Even though the wind had dropped, they were nervous, milling around their bed ground, unwilling to settle.

"I want three men on the herd tonight. Just in case." Bob took a plate and ladled stew into it. "Julio, you eat, then go out and send Tony and Trini in for supper. I'll be right behind you."

"Fill your bellies now," Solly said. "Then git out your slickers. No sense waitin' till heaven opens up."

Thunder rumbled in the distance, and the dawn light

was diffused, greenish, but the rain held off. They moved out slowly, covering several miles before the first drops spattered in the dust.

Livvy looked around, as nervous as the mares. "I don't like this," she said to Sim.

"Me, neither. But we can't fight what we can't see." He hitched the collar of his slicker higher.

"Yet," she said.

Then they saw it—a high, black funnel that appeared and spiraled toward them, gaining speed and strength.

"Down there!" Sim's shout was blotted out by the tornado's roar, but Livvy was already heading for the protection of a stream tucked between high banks.

Out of the corner of her eye, she saw the panicked mares and riders scattering, and then Belle, as terrified as the rest, leaped down the bank and went to her knees. Livvy threw herself off, avoiding the scrambling hoofs, aware only of wind and the howling menace that was sweeping toward them.

"All right?" Sim shouted in her ear.

She nodded. Talk was useless. Life hung in the balance—his, hers, the others' who were fighting their own desperate fight on a battleground she could not see.

Overhead, saplings bent and broke; branches were torn from the small trees that had their roots in the bed of the stream. Sim reached out and took her hand in a strong grip. *As if,* she thought, *he can hold me here. Or we'll both get taken.*

She didn't want to die, sucked up into the maw of the gigantic column of air, spun around, torn apart like a toy, a corn dolly and expendable. Closing her eyes, she began to pray, a simple prayer of one word. *Please. Please.*

Suddenly there was silence—a silence so deep she heard the sigh of a ragged leaf, falling beside her. "It's over," she said, awed by the fact that her prayer had been answered and by the sight of Sim, his face plastered with mud. "You should see yourself."

"I bet I don't look half as funny as you." He laughed, then held her, kissing the dirt from her cheeks and mouth.

Together they climbed out and stood looking at an almost empty landscape, scarred by the path the tornado had taken. A hundred yards downstream, Belle was cropping grass, but, of the rest, there was no sign.

Sim said: "Jesus!"

"They have to be somewhere. They can't have all disappeared. We can ride double and go look." Livvy whistled, and Belle lifted her head and nickered, then came toward them. "If we're lucky," Livvy added, "the Cordells all got swept away."

"Nobody's that lucky." Sim ran a careful hand down Belle's legs, then tightened the saddle cinch and let out the stirrups. "Any ideas where to start?" he asked, swinging Livvy up behind him.

"They were all headed that way, last I saw." She pointed over his shoulder.

They went several miles, sweeping back and forth,

finding some of the mares gathered in a hollow. Others were spread out, grazing but still restless, moving off at their approach.

"¡*Hola, Señor* Sim!" From the hill beyond the dip, Julio and Tony appeared, grins of welcome on their dark faces. "We think you were lost!"

"We thought you was. Where's the others?"

"Here, *señor*, and more of the horses. We go now to find the rest. Maybe." Tony shook his head. "Mother of God, but never have I seen such a thing as that. I think we all be killed."

"We were damned lucky. Anybody see my horse?"

"No, *señor*. Only our own. But horses we have."

"Bareback's not my style for more than a couple miles," Sim said. "Where's Solly? He's got my old saddle in the wagon."

"He is not with us."

Livvy hopped off Belle. "Take my saddle," she said. "I'll stay here with Belle and keep watch on this bunch."

It made sense, except Sim wasn't leaving her alone. "Stay with her, Tony," he ordered. "We'll be back in a while . . . I hope."

Tony nodded. Like the rest, he'd just as soon shoot a Cordell as look at him. "She will be safe," he promised, and watched with admiration as Livvy improvised a hackamore from her lariat and jumped on Belle's bare back, as at ease as if she had grown there. A woman to make any man proud, he thought. And a woman he would defend with his life.

65

● ● ●

Cameron Cordell searched the prairie through his field glasses, seeing stray mares but no sign of riders. He wondered if the tornado had done for his prey, and felt cheated at the thought. He wanted to see the girl squirm, wanted her to beg before he killed her, and the same with that husband of hers. He'd picked up Belle's tracks days before, and now he had only one thought in mind.

"What d'you see, Pa?" Ike was at his elbow, breathing hard through his mouth like his mother used to do.

"Hosses," Cameron said, irritated. "That's it."

Ike giggled. "Mebbe we oughta have us a little roundup. Them mares'll fetch a fancy price."

That was Ike, never able to keep his mind on what was important, always looking for an easy buck. "Shut up," Cameron said. "We'll worry about that after we've done what we come for."

"What if that thing killed 'em?"

"That's what we're gonna find out."

By evening the men had rounded up most of the scattered herd, but there was still no sign of Solly.

Bob's face was haggard with strain and exhaustion. "Looks like we tighten our belts and try again tomorrow," he said to the group, standing around him. "If we can't find Solly, I'll ride over to that herd west of us and see if I can't get help from the trail boss. Then we'll just get on with it. We lost about thirty head, some

66

of 'em dead, but there's no time to go look for the others." He had come across the carcasses of several mares and two colts and hoped he'd never see that again—necks broken, legs snapped like matchsticks, eyes and noses already clogged with flies.

"Anybody see our friends?" Sim asked.

Bob shook his head. "Nope. But that don't mean much. You and me will take first watch. The rest of you get some sleep." He mounted his horse and rode out, shoulders sagging.

Livvy awoke in the morning, sick from hunger and scolding herself. She'd been hungry before, too many times to count, and had survived like she would now. There was food all around them—birds' eggs, roots, rabbits, and prairie chickens, plenty for the clever hunter.

Quietly she got to her feet. No sense announcing her plan. They'd all squelch it, fearing for her safety. She almost screamed when Sim wrapped his fingers around her ankle. "Where you off to?" he asked.

"No place."

"Come on, Liv. Tell the truth."

He'd always been able to read her, and now was no different. "To get breakfast," she said. "I'm surprised none of you thought of it."

"Don't you get out of sight of camp," he warned. "Better yet, wait till Bob gets back."

She stamped her foot. "This is silly! We sit here and starve and wait to be picked off like ducks in a pond, wait for somebody to feed us like we're baby birds. We're not helpless. Let's do something! Anything rather than sit here."

She was in a rage, not uncommon. Sim had weathered a few of them while growing up, and, if he were honest, she'd usually been in the right.

"I'll come with you," he said.

"Then hurry up. I'm hungry." She pulled on her boots and stalked off.

"Git up there you lead-bellied, no-good mules. Haul your asses!" The shout cut through the crystal air like a knife, as Solly drove top speed into camp.

"What happened?"

"Where you been?"

The questions flew, and Solly grinned, his teeth shining white in his dark face.

"I been out there hidin' from the breath of Satan. Me and the mules got down in a cañon and let that devil blow over, and then I had to figure where you all had got to, but I'm here now, and I bet you're glad of it. Breakfast's comin' right up."

"Amen," Sim said, and the others echoed him.

They crossed the Canadian. Fort Supply lay ahead, and the last hard push into Dodge City before moving on to Nebraska. Livvy found herself longing for rude civilization—a bath, a bed with just Sim and herself and no need to be quiet about lovemaking.

Although driving horses was different from trailing cattle, the distance seemed endless, the routine boring,

68

as unlike her Comanche days as sun and moon, and she found herself short-tempered, unable to forget the threat of the Cordells somewhere behind. Of Indians, they'd seen no sign.

They rested the herd on good grass near Fort Supply, and Livvy, Solly, Bob, and Sim rode in to get supplies and information.

"A bath for me," Livvy told them. "You all can go shopping and gossip." Funny how quickly she'd got used to regular bathing, the pleasures of warm water and unlimited soap.

She lay back in the tub, eyes closed, thinking of nothing in particular but vaguely disturbed by a thought she couldn't grasp, that danced behind consciousness like swamp fire. Then in an instant she knew. Her eyes flew open in astonishment as she looked down at herself, at the whiteness of her body, the unaccustomed fullness of her breasts.

"Well," she said out loud, "well, fancy that! I wonder how Sim's going to take bein' a daddy so soon." She lay back again, laughing in pure delight.

The post trader, Purington, was helping Sim and Solly load supplies while warning them of the dangers that lay ahead. He was a grim-looking man, dark-haired, with a toothpick dangling out of his mouth.

"There's been Injun trouble lately," he said. "That upstart Wolf Shit's at it again. And ain't that a name for the books?" He spat without removing the pick. "Seems like he needs to make himself look good after that trouble at 'Dobe Walls a few years back. Lost plenty of face in that one. But he's got a bunch of braves off the reservation, and they been raidin' and causin' trouble all along. You best keep your eyes open. Those hosses of yours'll look like a prize to a bunch of Injuns."

"Thanks for the warning. We survived a tornado, I reckon we can survive him," Sim said as he counted out payment. "Ready, Solly?"

"As I'll ever be."

Purington shifted the toothpick from one side of his mouth to the other. "Somebody's been runnin' guns to the bastards, too, just so you know. Best keep yours to hand."

Livvy joined them, her hair washed and shining, a smile on her face. "And keep her out of sight," he added.

"Out of whose sight?" she wanted to know.

"Injun trouble. Maybe," Sim answered.

"Well," she said, "you've got me along."

"Yeah. That's what bothers me." He boosted her up to the wagon seat, missing the scowl that replaced her smile.

If it came to trouble, she'd try her best to handle it, and without fighting. When it came to white men, they shot first, then parlayed. The problem, as she saw it, was fear and hatred, a bad combination that was true for both sides. She'd just use common sense and courtesy, and hope her strategy worked. Telling Sim about fatherhood would have to wait.

They crossed the Cimarron without incident and camped for the night. A full moon rose, illuminating the land, touching the bodies of the mares with silver. Watching them, Livvy thought they seemed magical, like creatures out of myth, all splendid curves and flowing tails, and legs made for running, the equivalent of wings.

"No trouble tonight," Bob said, interrupting her half dream. "No varmints are gonna hit us when we can see to pick 'em off."

No, she thought, *not tonight, but maybe tomorrow*. They were out there. She could feel them, her people, waiting with the patience of expert hunters. When they came, it would be up to her to avoid a slaughter.

In the morning she asked to ride point with Sim. "I've eaten enough dust this trip," she said as an excuse.

Bob laughed. The closer they got to Kansas, the better he felt. "Reckon you're right. Go on ahead, but keep your eye peeled."

They had just topped the first rise north of the river when she saw them—a hundred mounted warriors on the crest of the next hill.

"Injuns!" Sim put a loop on the bell mare and swung her left. "Circle the herd!" To Livvy he yelled: "Git out of here! Go back with the drag!"

Instead, she kicked Belle into a trot and headed out, one hand raised in the sign of peace.

One of the braves left the group and rode toward her, his arm up in the same gesture. He was a Comanche, but she didn't know him, and didn't much care for what she could read on his face.

"What band are you?" she asked when they were facing each other.

He didn't answer her question, but said: "You speak our tongue. Why?"

"I lived with the Quahadis for six years. Stone Ear and Turns Around were my adopted parents."

Changing the subject again, he said: "You have fine horses. The whites have killed and stolen many of ours. We want to look and see if you have Comanche horses."

It was a trick, of course, and the man made her uneasy. "We have no horses but our own," she countered. "We are moving them to the land above the Platte."

He waved his arm, signaling his braves to surround the herd. "We will look," he said.

"There will be shooting." Livvy spoke as calmly as she could. "My husband and his brother are good, honest men, but, if you try to take our horses, they will shoot. Then the Army will come and make more trouble for you and your people. Come and meet my husband, and we will talk."

He was silent a minute, thinking, then nodded, gesturing again to his braves. "We will talk."

She turned Belle, and he followed. "What is your name?" she asked.

"I am Ish-Tai."

With an effort, Livvy kept a straight face. *Wolf Shit!*

72

she thought. *How in God's name had he gotten The People to believe in him, follow him with a name like that?*

Still, his braves had held back at his signal. Obviously he had some power she hadn't heard about, and he wasn't the least cowed by the sight of Bob, Sim, and the others, armed and ready.

"One pony for each brave," he said. "Or we take the whole herd."

Livvy translated, and Bob exploded. "Tell him to get the hell out, or we'll sic the Army on what's left of 'em!"

She knew better than to translate that. She said: "These horses are those of his father, a big chief who has never done your people any harm, and a friend of the Great White Father in Washington. If he loses his horses, the Army will come and kill all yours."

Ish-Tai snorted. "The Great White Father lies and is no better than any other white man. If the Army comes for us, we will fight them."

Sim's anger was getting the best of him. The Comanche's attitude was too damned arrogant, and he didn't like the way he was looking at Livvy. "Tell him I'll shoot him down if he doesn't haul his ass out of here."

Ish-Tai's expression showed that he understood Sim's threat. He swung his horse, ready to make a run for it, and Bob muttered: "Now you did it. Keep your mouth shut and let Liv do the talkin'."

Livvy's attention was caught by a lone rider on a

flashy warbonnet paint, approaching from the west at a trot, and her heart leaped as she recognized her friend.

The Comanche drew up beside Ish-Tai. "What the hell is going on here?" he said, as near as Livvy could translate his words.

"That's Quanah," she whispered to Sim.

Hearing her, Quanah turned and looked her over carefully while she held her breath. "Little Redbird. Is it you?" he asked.

"It's been a long time," she said, smiling. "I have missed my friends and my brother. This is my husband and his brother." She repeated what she'd told Ish-Tai, and, as she went on, Quanah's face grew serious.

He had little use for Ish-Tai since he'd lied to The People, inspired them to hope with his tales of the sun dance, then promised he'd cough up magic bullets for them to kill the buffalo hunters at Adobe Walls. Faced with a dozen dead comrades, he'd turned coward, blaming a warrior who had killed a skunk the morning of the battle with breaking his medicine.

"Enough!" Quanah said to Livvy. To Ish-Tai, he said: "These are my friends, and this woman is a friend of our people. Take the men and leave."

In case they disobeyed and came back that night, he said to Livvy: "I will ride with you a while."

"You have had much trouble," Livvy said as they moved, side-by-side, up the trail. "I'm sorry for it."

His eyes were sad. "The buffalo are going, and so are we, Little Redbird. It is the end of one time and the beginning of another."

74

"And Stone Ear? Turns Around?"

He shook his head. "Both dead. They were old. And hungry. The winter was hard, and I couldn't help them. I can't help myself. The rules are all changed."

She held back the tears that came at the thought of her adoptive parents, at the hopelessness in her friend's voice.

"Will you eat with us tonight?" she said, changing the subject. At least she could feed him, give him back some of the kindness he'd shown to her.

"And tomorrow, too," he said with a half smile, acknowledging his situation without losing pride.

He left them at the Arkansas, and they watched until he stopped on the horizon, waved, and disappeared.

Bob let out a whistle. "Hate to say it, but that's a fine man. It's a good thing you were along, little Sister. You saved our bacon for sure. Speakin' of bacon, he ate enough for any ten of us."

"He was hungry," Livvy said softly. "His people are starving."

Solly shook his head. "It's a sorry business. But he turned out almost good enough to be white like us." He wondered why everyone laughed.

"I'll drink to that one," Sim said. "When we get to Dodge, let's tie one on. I'm ready."

The bluffs rose a hundred feet above the creek, sculpted by wind and rain and thousands of years of erosion as the stream cut deeper into the prairie.

Livvy and Sim stood looking up at the striated cliffs, she searching for words to tell him her news, and Sim giving thanks they'd come this far without confrontation.

"A few more days, we'll be in Dodge," he said. "I'll turn the Cordell business over to the sheriff, and we'll have a little celebration. Dinner at the Dodge House. The works."

For herself, she would be sorry to leave Indian Territory behind, for its beauty as well as its sorrows and fear. She slipped her hand into his and leaned against him.

"I . . . there's something I have to tell you," she began, then faltered. How best to say it, the secret she'd withheld for several days.

Her eyes danced, but there was purpose behind them, and he smiled at her. "Good or bad?"

"Oh, good. It's just . . . well, you're going to be a daddy one of these months, so we'll really have something to celebrate."

He didn't move. A daddy! Him! He remembered his vision of himself and Livvy grown old with children and grandchildren, and then saw himself as he was— quick to anger, quick to strike, with never a thought about how his actions would affect others. He'd married Livvy without regard for the future or the responsibilities that would come with a family of his own. In that minute his boyhood ended. In that minute Sim Hightower, hell-raiser, avenger, reckless youth vanished. He took a deep breath and whistled as he let it out. "I'm glad," was all he said before he kissed her.

Then the thought of her riding all the way to Nebraska hit him hard. If something happened to her, he'd be powerless to help, and the men wouldn't be any better. If he lost her—or the baby—he wouldn't be able to stand it.

Swallowing hard, he said: "When we get to Dodge, I'm wiring Jude. You're going the rest of the way on the train, and he can meet you."

Livvy's mouth dropped open. "The train! I'm not takin' any train. I'm fine. If I hadn't told you, you'd never have known, so just pretend you didn't hear me, Sim. That's final."

"We can't chance it."

"We!" she shouted. "It's *me*. It's my body, and I'm tellin' you I'm all right and will be."

"Honey. . . ."

She was really angry now. "Don't honey me. And don't start treatin' me like I'm made out of glass. I've been riding all my life, lived through things you don't want to hear. Another month isn't goin' to hurt me."

"And I'm tellin' you I won't let you risk it. *That's* final, too."

He could, she supposed, put her bodily on the train and probably would. When his jaw got set the way it was, arguing with him was useless. Maybe after he'd cooled down and had a chance to think, she'd be able to convince him. But she was too mad to say anything rational.

"Oh, go on and leave me alone," she said, pushing him away.

"Liv. . . ."

"I said leave me be."

"If that's how you want it. But you're goin' on that train." He walked down the hill toward camp, his boot heels digging deep holes in the soft ground.

She saw herself a prisoner in petticoats, dress, and bonnet in a hot, stinking railroad car while, outside, the land, which was as necessary to her as Sim, lured. Oh, she'd survive the way she always had, by holding on to that self that was locked deep inside, a kernel of belief and pride that was indestructible, but she should have kept her secret, should never have spoken about what was still invisible.

"Damn it! Damn it!" Bending down, she picked up a stone and threw it with all her strength into the water, and watched as the ripples spread out and vanished. Then she sat and pulled off her boots, rolled the ragged edges of her pants to her knees, and stepped into the creek.

Her own face stared up at her, a face she hardly recognized, burned brown by the sun, the eyes bright with anger. For the first time in years she wondered about her real mother, the woman who had borne her and who had died with a Comanche arrow through her breast. What had she felt in those last, fearful moments, what ferocity had lent her the strength to call out to her daughter—"Run, Livvy, run!"—before her own blood choked her?

It was the need, inborn, to protect the child. Sim had understood, but she had not. As a mother, she had a duty, an obligation to the new life. After all, Sim had been right, and now she'd have to swallow her anger and her pride and tell him so.

"Damn it!" she repeated. She hated being in the wrong, and apologies came hard. "Just get it over with."

"That's right, gal. We'll get it over with quicker'n you think." The arm around her neck was unyielding, cutting off her breath. She twisted, squirmed, kicked back hard, then realized she'd left her boots on the sand.

Whoever it was had clapped a hand over her mouth, so she bit down into the flesh and held on, fury overcoming terror.

"Bitch!" It came out a snarl. "I'll fix you for that. I'll screw you into the ground just afore I cut your throat." He tore his hand loose, slapped her hard, then grabbed her hair, and pulled her toward him.

Dizzy, struggling for a breath that wouldn't come, she recognized Ike Cordell. Oh, she knew him—half crazy and meaner than a snake. He'd rape her and then take his time with the knife.

Fight! She had to fight! For herself . . . the baby . . . her family! She had to get free. If only she could get a breath.

The hatred in her eyes inflamed him. To him, she was only a squaw, not one of the high and mighty Hightowers. Who knew how many Indians had had her before they tossed her out? And what gave her the right

79

to look at him like he was dirt? Yet it was plain she'd kill him if she got the chance.

He slapped her again, harder this time, and the blow knocked her to the ground. She lifted her head, half-conscious, panting, her lungs and throat on fire. Strong as she was, she was no match for him, and her gun was in her boot out of reach. Moaning, she lifted herself on her hands and knees, only to be pulled up by her belt and slammed back to the ground, hands spread out in front of her, fingers resting on the toe of her right boot.

She would need to be quick. One chance was all she would get, and even at that she'd need luck and a clear head. *Stay still*, she told herself. *Don't move until you're sure*. She tipped the boot toward her.

Ike's foot slammed into the small of her back and stayed there. "You won't need that where you're goin'. Lay still."

By turning her head, she could see him out of the corner of her eye, unbuttoning his pants, balanced on one foot.

"You're not the man your Pa is," she said. "I never heard of him raping women."

"Shut up!" Ike's mouth stayed open, and he was breathing hard.

She had it now. Her chance wouldn't come again. Like a snake she twisted, turned, pulled the trigger, and was stunned to hear a second blast almost simultane-ously. *Sim?* she wondered. Then Cameron Cordell stalked out of the bushes and came toward her, his .45 aimed at her heart.

"You gonna rape me, too?" she asked, taking a chance, stalling for time.

He stared at her from four feet away. "I don't hold with that."

"Then shoot me and get it over with. But I'll take you down with me."

Cameron considered his chances. There was no doubt she meant it, and the Derringer was a nasty weapon. "You killed my boys," he said.

"We can argue about him." She pointed to Ike, his shirt stained red. "He tried to rape me. The other one I caught rustling. He shot first."

"That the truth?"

"Yes."

"I don't believe no Injun."

She raised the Derringer higher. "I'm as white as you, old man. And a damn' sight better than the trash you bred."

She was fearless. In spite of himself, he admired her, sprawled there with rage in every inch, the Derringer steady. She was right about his bad seeds. The truth didn't hurt like it once had.

"Truce," he said.

She didn't blink. "Put the gun away."

"I ain't stupid, missy."

"Neither am I."

"I been thinkin' these last couple days," he said slowly. "About how if we keep up, there won't be a Cordell or a Hightower left." He nudged Ike's foot with the toe of his boot. "Ike was no good, and Roy and

Buzz wasn't much to brag about. But I got one good son left, and I'd like to know he'll be here after I'm gone."

Standing there, he looked like what he was, a fighter, a father who protected his own, and she understood just as she understood that the power to stop the feud lay in her hands.

"Let's end it then," she said. "For once and all. There's been enough killing, and Nolan and Willa think the same. You want your son. They want theirs, and I want mine. And my husband."

"What about the rest of 'em? They gonna agree?"

"What about the other one who was with you? Is he gonna come in shootin'?"

"Drunk, up at Reighard's road ranch. He ain't got nothin' to say about what I decide."

"All right then. Let's go down and talk it out," she said. "You and me."

Hell, he'd be a fool if he believed that one. "I ain't walkin' into no ambush."

She took a chance and put the Derringer in her pocket, then picked up her boots. "I reckon you're not a back-shooter. I'll go in first. You can come or not, but, if you don't, sooner or later you'll be layin' in the ground with the rest."

He thought about the graves, too many of them, about misplaced trust, and his wife, mourning Dave, keeping little Lyle close to home out of fear and desperation. He thought about himself and Nolan, growing old, passing on a violent and useless legacy.

Abruptly he shoved his pistol into its holster. "We'll go down together, missy," he said.

She sensed rather than felt the tremor in her belly, a flutter like moth wings, an affirmation of life in the wake of death, and she held out her hand.

"Amen," she said, smiling. "Amen."

Aunt Addy and the Cattle Rustler

My Aunt Addy came here from Texas in '73. "Too crowded back there," was the way she always put it, and I believed her because even this country started to fill up once the railroad came through.

I have to say, though, that Aunt Addy and Uncle Henry helped the population along, with six kids of their own and me and my sis raised with them. We were kin, taken in when our parents died.

"We'll make do," Aunt Addy said at the time, and that, as I learned, was her motto. Through it all, she "made do."

My sis and I hadn't been at the homestead for more than a few years when Aunt Addy made the first in a series of startling decisions. We were boarding the schoolteacher that year, Miss Lemon by name, and a falser name nobody ever had. Miss Lemon was as sweet as wild honey, and everybody loved her, especially us kids who fell all over ourselves trying to please her.

As it turned out, Uncle Henry lost his head over her, too, right there in the house that was spilling over with his own kids and his wife, although she, like as not, was out on horseback doing his job.

Uncle Henry just wasn't practical. No—what he was, was a fool. He had two homesteads, one in his name and one in his wife's, and a passel of mouths to feed, and what he did was to read and dream and putter

84

around the house and garden, talking to us kids, teaching us our letters and a little bit of history and religion on the side. We loved it, followed him around like chicks, but it was Aunt Addy we went to for advice, or help, or anything practical. It was Aunt Addy who taught us how to make do in the wilderness, where to hide in thunderstorms, how to take a prickly pear and boil it into a poultice for snakebite, and when to plant and harvest. She taught us all to ride and cut calves, too, and to brand them, AH on the left hip. It was Aunt Addy who thought up the idea of sewing silver coins under the skin of her calves' necks. Brands could be changed, she said, but only we knew about those coins. It's a trick that's been used since, but it was her idea at the start.

Anyhow, there was Aunt Addy out riding the range, leaving Uncle Henry and the teacher at home to recite poetry and look into each other's eyes, and pretty soon they headed off to the barn and the privacy of the hayloft. But, as I said, Uncle Henry was a fool. He couldn't expect to hide his infatuation from eight kids and a sharp-eyed wife for long, and he didn't.

Aunt Addy came back early one day, her horse having stepped in some cholla, and, when she led it into the barn, the first thing she saw was the ruffled petticoat our Miss Lemon was so proud of. Only Miss Lemon wasn't wearing it. She'd left it hanging over the edge of the loft in her haste, and it was there, fluttering like a flag in the breeze.

Aunt Addy went up the ladder quick as a snake and

found what she suspected: Uncle Henry in his shirt and shoes and not much else, and Miss Lemon minus her fine lace petticoat. Addy chased the two of them down just as they were, while us kids gaped and sniggered and formulated ideas depending on how old we were and how much we knew at the time.

Aunt Addy followed more slowly, carrying Uncle Henry's pants over her arm. She went across the yard after them and into the house.

What followed was a scene from one of those melodramas, with all of us lined up against the windows, and Miss Lemon inside swooning while Uncle Henry bent over her, showing his bare bottom to the sky.

Aunt Addy stood there, grim as death, arms folded across her chest. Finally she spoke. "Henry," she said, "get your pants on before your brains get cold."

And when Henry said—"Now, Addy."—in that sweet way of his, she said: "Don't 'now Addy' me. You get your pants on, and then you get your things, and you and your Miss Lemon here get off my ranch."

Uncle Henry hopped on one foot, pulling on his pants. "This here's my home, Addy," he said. He hopped on the other foot.

"No more, it isn't," she said. "A man uses his house as a brothel don't have much other use for it." She frowned at Miss Lemon who was sobbing into her handkerchief. "And a teacher who indulges in fornication ain't much of a teacher. You been teaching all my boys, or just this one?"

Miss Lemon sobbed harder.

Aunt Addy said: "The two of you are as much use as tits on a mule. Be off my property before sundown. I've had a bellyful of your children. Time you started on someone else."

They left, Miss Lemon leaning on Uncle Henry and carrying her suitcase. Uncle Henry was carrying a trunk full of books. Like I said, he wasn't practical.

We all lined up by the gate to see them go. He shook our hands, each in turn, and told us to be good and help our mother. I guess he forgot I wasn't one of his, because he said the same to me and patted me on the head.

Aunt Addy cooked a big pot of beans and ham hocks for supper that night, and opened a jar of piccalilli, and made sourdough biscuits and a dried apple pie, and she sat in Uncle Henry's place at the head of the old pine table and looked at us. After we'd sopped up the last bean and eaten the pie down to the dish, she gave us our orders.

We were, she said, going to make do. We had our fields of cane and corn, our garden, our beef cattle, our hogs and chickens. We had our backs and our hands and the wits God gave us, and, thank God, none of us took after Henry. She assigned each of us jobs, the girls getting the kitchen and housework, the boys the hoeing, planting, and herding. We'd sell beeves to the Army and to the reservation and the local market. Produce, too, what we could spare. There was to be no complaining, no shirking, no tomfoolery. And, she added, being as we were near the main road, we'd take in travelers who wanted a bed for the night.

"Rustlers, too?" I asked, for rustlers were what we saw most of, and the posses behind them.

"Rustlers, too," she said, "and nary a word to anyone."

She lit up one of Uncle Henry's cigars that he'd left behind in his rush, and we gaped at her in astonishment. "Now this is my place," she said, sitting back and exhaling, "I don't aim to smoke behind the barn." She stared us down and returned to her train of thought. "Rustlers especially. If we're good to them, they'll leave us alone out of gratitude."

It sounded like good sense to me, though I'd rather have been on horseback than hoeing the fields. The thing about her plan was, she made it sound like an adventure, like something exciting that only grown folks did and into which we were being initiated, and we all rose to the bait as, I'm sure, she knew we would. In our beds that night we whispered about rustlers and outlaws as if a new world had opened up, and in a way it had.

Word about Uncle Henry got 'round pretty fast because the school had to close and people wanted to know why. Aunt Addy told them, too, straight-out. She never did beat about the bush like most women. To those who asked about him, she said: "He's gone and good riddance. Now I can stick to business."

She did, too. She worked harder than any man I ever saw, not because she was driven to it, but because she purely loved it. She told me once she never did feel right except on horseback, working cattle, or just riding for the pleasure of it.

"It has something to do with freedom," she said, and then she laughed and said, me being a boy, I wouldn't understand.

I thought I did, though. Once in a while I had a day with nothing to do, and I'd go off into the mountains or down onto the flat, and I'd get to feeling wild with all that space to move in. Sometimes I'd take the Mexican pony, Chico, and we'd run just for the fun of it, and no one to tell us to stop. So I thought I pretty well understood Aunt Addy and her love of the outside, of having a good horse under her that knew what she wanted.

Life went on. Uncle Henry's absence didn't change anything much. He'd never been the heart of the place. We all did our share, and willingly, too, because we were happy and didn't want to lose the ranch or be split up or sent away from Aunt Addy.

After a while, travelers started stopping. All kinds of people: men headed for the silver and copper mines, prospectors searching for gold, families looking for a likely place to settle. We had some Mormons once, and a family of black folks, and I can remember staring at that family, never having seen anybody that color.

"Mind your manners, boy," Aunt Addy said to me as I inched closer to see them. She called all of us "boy," because she said she couldn't remember so many names. It didn't signify a lack of affection. We just took it for granted she knew who we were and loved us with or without names.

About the Mormons she had a little more to say. The man had two wives, pretty women, and a bunch of children. "Henry was born to the wrong religion," she said when she saw them. Then she smiled kind of grim. "At least one of them gets a rest once in a while. Maybe there's something in it, after all." But she didn't talk much to them because, she said, down deep she felt bigamy was indecent.

Illegality didn't bother her, however. We put up plenty of rustlers and enjoyed their company, too. Generally they were nicer and more polite than regular folks. They helped wash up after supper, and sometimes they'd tell us kids tales as good as anything in books. Some of them even passed out a coin or two for grooming their horses or making some small repair to their tack.

Black Bob Beaufort was a regular visitor, partly because he had a run between Mexico and the Peak where he branded and hid out his stolen cattle, and partly because he was sweet on Aunt Addy. She was a handsome woman, tall and black-haired, and she had a way of moving, quick and sure, that made people look at her.

She had a soft spot for Black Bob, too, because like all strong women she had a weakness for a gentle man. She never could resist one weaker than she was, and with Black Bob she had a prime candidate. She bossed him, bullied him, sometimes even told him how to pull a job. She had the planning kind of mind that he lacked.

"So blamed innocent," she said once. "How a man

like that ever came to rustling I can't understand."

However he came to it, Aunt Addy was quick to see its uses.

She was pining for a Thoroughbred bull because at that time ranchers were importing all kinds of strains trying to improve their stock. But because there were so many of us, we never had much cash. We ate most of what we produced, and the extra got sold or traded for whatever else we needed. So, though she had her heart set on a good bull, she went without. Until one night on the back porch when she said as much to Black Bob.

Sometimes the two of them would sit there after supper, smoking cigars in the dark and talking about this and that with all of us tucked away somewhere nearby to listen.

That morning Aunt Addy had hid Bob under her bed when a posse come by looking for him, and she was chuckling over her success and puffing away contented, and then all of a sudden she let out a sigh that would've torn a stronger man than Beaufort in half.

He turned all sweet like he could and moved closer to her. "What's the matter, Addy?" he asked.

She sighed again. Even in the dark I could see the gleam in her eye and was surprised he couldn't. "Nothing," she said.

"Got to be something to make you sigh like that."

"I was just wishing I had me a good bull," she said, sounding so wistful I had to smile.

"A bull," he said. "What for?"

That was too much for her. "Use your head, man,"

91

she snapped. "What do folks usually use bulls for?"

"Oh," he said. And then: "But you got a bull."

"Not a nice Hereford, I don't," she said. "Not like the ones Ike Tyler's got. Everybody's breeding up but me. I've got scrubs. That's all."

He chewed that one over a while. Then he said: "Addy, I can get you a bull."

"I don't want no stolen animal," she said. "Lying's one thing. Taking a bull with someone else's brand on, is another."

He thought again. I swear I could hear his brains creak. "What if it don't have a brand?" he asked.

"That's different. Anybody leaves a good bull out unbranded don't deserve him."

Black Bob rode out at first light. When he'd been gone for four weeks, Aunt Addy got restless.

"I knew it," she said one morning over breakfast. "The dang' fool's got himself killed or hanged, and it's my fault. I put him up to it."

"What'd you put him up to?" I asked.

"Stealing a bull," she said.

"He does it all the time," I said, trying to comfort her. "That's how he makes a living."

"Lord God," she said. "That don't mean he won't get caught." She lit a cigar. "I should've gone out and rustled my own."

"Aunt Addy!" I said.

She remembered it was me she was talking to and laughed like she was trying to erase what she'd just said. "I'm joking, boy. You know that."

But I kept thinking of how she'd gone all sad and soft that night on the porch, and I figured she hadn't been joking at all.

That night, after supper, Aunt Addy called a conference.

"It's come down to it," she said. "I need a bull, and I guess I'll have to work for it. If you all can handle things here, I'm going to town and get work in the saloon."

"The saloon!" we said.

Evie, the oldest said: "Ma, you can't work in a saloon. It ain't right."

"If I do it, it'll be right," Aunt Addy said.

"I'll go work in the saloon," Evie said, with hope in her voice, I thought.

Aunt Addy gave her a long look from under those straight black eyebrows of hers. "No, miss, you won't," she said. "You'll stay here and keep yourself decent."

She sighed. "There's another way."

"What?" we asked.

"I can sell Acorn to Ike Tyler."

Acorn was Aunt Addy's cutting mare, and every rancher in the county had his eye on her—six years old, smart and strong, and all over the smooth tan color of an acorn. Working cattle with that mare was a treat. You could close your eyes, sit back, and just hold on. She did the rest.

The thought of trading Acorn for a big, dumb, mean-tempered bull was too much for me. I had another idea. I raised my hand, and Aunt Addy looked at me.

"What is it, boy?"

"You oughtn't to sell her," I said. "What you ought to do is, well, you know that big gray stud horse of Ike Tyler's?"

She nodded once, quick.

"You ought to take the mare over there some night. Get you a good colt. Sell the colt and keep the mare. It'll take a while, but you can always get a bull. Thing is, you'll never get another Acorn."

Her gray eyes narrowed to slits. She thought a while. Then she said: "Boy, you got sense for such a little bugger. I wish you were one of mine."

I turned red with pleasure. Praise from Aunt Addy was rare.

She said: "You think you can handle that?"

I nodded.

"Good," she said. "We'll keep a check on her. First night she's ready, you'll go."

And I did, in the light of a tracker's moon. I remember that night like it was written in my head—the whippoorwill crying near the wash, the coyotes singing in the hills, and a flock of ducks flying right across the moon in a world so still I could hear the whistle of their wings.

Something began to ache inside me that night, some hunger I didn't know I had or what it was for, only that I wished nothing would end, that I could stay in that moment forever, with the cottonwood trees white and twisted, the grass blowing like a woman's hair, and the smooth body of the mare moving under me like running water. I remember it all, even how they looked, mare and stud, bigger than horses, more like two clouds come together in the sky, straining to be together, to pull apart.

When he was done, the stud stood there, slick with sweat and shining as if he was carved out of some white stone. His ears stuck up into the darkness over the heavy curve of his neck, and he whinnied so loud the mountain rang with it all the way home, making the mare quiver between my knees.

After that we waited—for the mare to foal, for Black Bob to come back. Aunt Addy had given up on him, though she didn't say so out loud. She just went on making do.

One morning more than five months after he'd left, Bob came riding up the lane on the sorriest horse I'd ever seen. He was leading a critter that looked like it come straight out of the book of prophecies. White it was, and black-spotted, with black circles around its eyes, and a hump on its back like a camel. It had a big, floppy brisket that hung nearly to the ground, and a pair of crooked black horns that stuck out above dangling ears.

"What in tarnation's that?" yelled Aunt Addy, completely forgetting her worry.

"I brought you your bull," said Bob. He swung off the horse that stood there heaving, nose in the dust.

"That ain't no bull," she said. "You made a mistake. That's a spotted clown."

"It's a bull," he said. "Honest. It's a Brahma. I went

clear to Texas for him."

"You wasted your time, then," she said. "But I am glad to see you back."

He said: "Addy, take a look. It's a bull, all right."

She sniffed. "I can see that. But does he know what he's supposed to do with it?"

Like I said, Aunt Addy always spoke her mind. Not everybody could take her plain speaking, but Beaufort just grinned.

"Yep," he said. "Bet we left spotted calves clear across New Mexico."

"They'll track you down, Beaufort," she said, laughing. "They'll follow them spotted calves right to my door."

"Addy," he said, "I paid for him. Cash. Got him from a circus."

She blinked. "I believe it. I surely do. Do them spots wash off?"

"This here's an East Indian bull!" Bob roared. "He comes by those spots on his own, and he'll stand up to heat and drought better'n any old Hereford. You believe me, Addy. This here bull will get you good calves."

I looked at Beaufort who'd grown a curly black beard that clung to his gaunt cheeks like mistletoe to a juniper tree. I looked at the horse, skin and bones and not much else. I looked at the bull, fleshed-out, firm, not even in a sweat.

I said: "Aunt Addy, maybe he's right. Look at the critter. He's fresh as dew. Put one of your dimes in him and turn him loose."

She laughed. "Boy," she said, "he don't need a dime. He's got all them spots and a water bag on his back to boot."

But in the end she did all of it, even placed her brand, AH, carefully on his left hip. She turned him loose, but not before he'd chewed through the vegetable garden and climbed the porch steps to give her a lick with his big tongue.

She ended up having to lead him into the hills where the cows were. "For better or worse, I got me a trick bull," she said.

For better or worse, Aunt Addy got a lot of things in the years that followed. In the spring, Acorn foaled a slate gray stud colt, even-tempered, playful as a pup, and sound. Aunt Addy couldn't bring herself to part with him.

"Now I've got me a stud and a bull," she said. "I surely do."

And when the cows began to calve, they dropped tough little calves, some spotted, but nary a one with a hump, and they grew and put on weight almost from the air itself.

Black Bob took on a halo in her eyes. "All that time I thought he was a fool," she said, shaking her head.

Somehow she persuaded him to give up rustling and settle down in our bunkhouse. I don't know what she promised him, but I suspect it was more than regular meals and thirty dollars a month.

Whatever it was, our lives went on, smooth as the passing of seasons. We did what had to be done and took pleasure in it, and pride. There was never time to be bored, but there was always time to look out over the land and fill up with joy, knowing it was ours and that we had, indeed, made do.

The Paseo

They still play in the plaza, those little girls in their brilliant dresses. The wind from the mountains scoops their skirts, and they laugh, twirl in it, hold down the billows mockingly as if they have something beneath that must not be exposed.

But one of them knows that soon she will have something to protect. She knows they will all grow tall and deep and holy, their bodies more precious than life. They will parade this plaza slowly, erect under the eyes of men, conscious of the pearls they bear in their darkness, conscious of sin, desirous of its consequences.

It is serious business, the *paseo*. In its prescribed motion the courses of lives are altered. It is a giant marketplace, offering not the chiles, blankets, jars, moccasins, jewelry of the weekday trade, but the bodies, the souls of women that have no price but that are, nonetheless, bartered over, traded, moved from one owner to the other. The women go eagerly or not so eagerly, wrapped around their pearls like oysters secreting splendor. They go, they grow old, they die, and their daughters practice the promenade, shriek in the wind, hold down dresses that wish to be wings.

The world runs on paradox. We wall up beauty behind adobe, then snarl and howl in the wilderness outside. We make animals of the least of us by telling him he is man, turn little girls into spiritual vessels at a time when honest laughter is precious, the light in their eyes beyond price.

However, I am as guilty as any, although once I was only observer, recorder of lives and scenes. I have been in this mud city for years, painting pictures, watching, listening, taking no part in the pageant, although I had my chances. Not long ago I was yellow-haired, considered handsome.

But to be bound up in that ritual would have been to lose some vitality I needed in my fingers, my heart. I chose, instead, to be father of mountains, of distances, of colors changing on the space of the desert. I was not free, but neither was I bound by voices, bodies, demands, only by my own urgings, my own needs. Another paradox, it seems. We suckle freedom in our mother's milk, yet, when we escape from her, we are bound to another.

These are things I think about in the night when I cannot see to paint, or when, as now, I think of the children, the little girls from the convent who walk and dream in the dust of the plaza. Once I walked among them. Now I, too, am walled behind adobe, cast out into the desert.

One child in particular attracted me. There was an aura of the unbreakable about her. I thought that the nuns would have a hard time convincing her of her guilt for Original Sin, that her mother, the widow who takes in boarders and who looks at me now with suspicion and disgust, would find it difficult to give her in marriage. The child, Dolores, would not be given. She would, instead, bestow herself like a queen as she bestowed on me her smiles. On me . . . El Chamiso. That is what she called me—after the yellow weed whose flowers hang, gray and drying on their stems all winter.

In the days before my fall, I talked to her often. I would go out and sit in the plaza on afternoons when I grew tired of my own company, of the voices of solitude. I would sit and let the giggles and gossip of little girls fly over me, would let her approach, dark eyes dancing in pointed face, aware of her daring, filled with mischief yet already powerful, already the queen followed by her handmaidens, giving audience to one man whose hair hung on his head like a winter weed, who revived in the presence of young laughter, who straightened to receive the honor of her attention.

Why was I not painting? she wanted to know the first time. Why was I there—jester in her court—when the snow had melted in the hills, the mountains stood up clear against the sky? The town, it seemed, marked its calendar by my comings and goings.

I told her I was growing too old to brave the winds of March. That I would wait for May, for the apples' time of blooming, and then I would pack my burro with brushes and paint, and be off into the high country.

She came closer then, put one hand on my knee in a gesture so childish yet so womanly I felt my heart leap in my chest, and even, God help me, a stirring in my loins.

What was it like, that high country? she asked. And

why could I not paint it from the images stored behind my eyes?

Her innocence could not recognize her words as a giving. When I began to tell her that the edges of memory are blurred, that what we recall is never what was there but only what we wish, she drew away, scornful that her gift had gone unnoticed. She ran, handmaidens behind her, small feet flashing under her striped skirt.

"El Chamiso!" she shouted from the far corner of the plaza where swirls of dust obscured her, made her brave. And they laughed, all of them, twittering like the sparrows that hide in the walls from the wind. But I did not mind. I am not bothered by names. One is as good as another, and, besides, was it not a title bestowed by a queen?

Soon though, I discovered her curiosity. She had never, in twelve years, been beyond the limits of the city, and she wanted to know about the world she had imagined. So I told her stories of the Indians in their pueblos, about how the desert looks in bloom. I told her of the beauty of loneliness with only the mesas for company, of the madness that came upon me when I tried to capture them on canvas. I talked to her as a man rarely talks to a woman, and she drank my words.

I waited in the plaza for them to come in a gaggle from school, moving clockwise as if in practice, although their steps were neither slow nor decorous and their voices were high-pitched, carrying. Some days I brought candy—peppermint, licorice, rock crystals, or those fiery little red drops that scorch the throat, the tongue as surely as chiles. How she sucked the air after one of those! How I watched her, wishing to take her in my arms, little queen that she was, to apologize, to learn her quiverings, her stillness.

Regardless of what they say about me now, I wanted only to hold childhood in my hands, to capture her in those moments before she turned woman, aware of self, body, games of pride. I wanted the pure vitality of that female animal to enter me, to come to me so that I could know it with these hands that have failed to capture what my eyes so clearly see.

Who has ever painted time? Arrested it? No one of whom I know, although many have tried. Day after day I have gone into the desert, have seen it, luminous and living before me, have mixed my colors and begun only to find it changed and changing again. To paint it is to indulge in mimicry, a hopeless attempt to possess what cannot be owned. It is enough to drive one mad.

So I sat, longing for the reality of that thin body between my hands, wanting the scent of hot young breath upon my face, the dazzle of tears. Wanting anything from her that spoke of living, that was unchanged for a day, an hour, a moment.

"You're wicked," she said, looking up at me in anger. Her lip trembled as she spoke, and I lost myself in its smoothness, in the perfection of color, pale rose like a petal. I saw it in a year, grown seductive—in twenty, cracked and dried from the sun—in forty, slack with dying. Inside myself I wept.

"Wicked," she repeated. I had tempted her like the serpent. I had burned her mouth and must do penance, make reparation.

"What?" I asked her. "What must I do?"

She thought a while, still and perfect between my knees, and then her mouth curved, her eyes danced. Every day for a week, she said, I must bring candy. Sweet candy of wonderful colors. And for her alone. Was that not a good penance?

I pretended to consider, nodding, weighing the thought like a fool, and all the time watching her delight. I noticed that her hair, which I had thought black, had fire in it, was overlaid by a sheen of gold. Beneath its tendrils, her face shone as if under a halo.

It was then that the idea came to me. It was an honest one and innocent. Truly. I wanted to capture that face on canvas. I wanted to paint that child on the brink of womanhood, the lily opening, hesitant, doomed, impelled by the fact that it lives. I wanted to paint that moment of trust when we believe that, because we are, life will not fail us. I wanted back my own moments of certainty.

I nodded at her. "Yes," I said. "It's a good penance. I'll do it. But you must do something for me."

She was smiling, victorious. "What?" she asked. "What, *viejo*?"

Old one. To her I was the old one, not the youth she would someday meet, watch under lowered lids in the circle of the *paseo*, lure to her side like a dark moth.

"You must ask your mama if I may paint you. Your portrait. Just as you are now."

I watched the idea grow in her, her enormous, slanted eyes catching fire like valleys in the dawn. I watched, dismayed, as the first glimmer of self-consciousness touched her and she began to view herself as an object of desire.

I cursed myself for my foolishness. No matter that in a year or two it would have come on its own. Like the serpent, I had placed knowledge squarely before her who believed in paradise.

When she spoke, her voice was still the clear treble of a young bird, but I was not fooled. The body speaks its own language, and hers had drawn inward, defensive, aware.

"Paint me?" she asked. "Why me?"

Why, indeed? "Never mind," I said. "It was a foolish notion. Go and play and I'll bring you candy tomorrow."

But she was not now to be put off by promises of treats, perhaps never again. "But I would like it," she said. "You'd make me beautiful, and everyone would see and talk about me."

Dreams galloped in her. I could feel them. Her hand was on my knee, insistent. "I'll hang on the wall like a great lady," she said, moving closer. "Please. I would like it. I will sit still for hours and hours, and not ask for candy. I will ask my mother tonight. I will tell her it is an honor." Her fingers tightened. "Please."

I thought that, after all, I was not an old man. Only mature. Only tired of wrestling abstractions from the unyielding body of earth. Perhaps it was time to come to terms with the beast within, to forget lines, shapes, colors, and learn the reality of the flesh.

I had already done the damage. I would paint her. I would make her beautiful as, indeed, she was, and I would make her conscious of me. Then, perhaps in a year, I would join the others circling her, as much a dog as they.

So dreams galloped, also, through me. So I, too, lost my innocence that clear day with the glitter of March around us, and the wind from the mountains tasting of snow.

But in this town nothing is secret. Gossip leaches from the walls. News is flashed by smiles, gestures, chance words, as if, beneath the surface, all are fastened together, a huge root with a thousand branches.

By the next morning, Luz, the silent woman who cooks for me, keeps my clothes in order, comes silently to my bed on those nights when the mountains bear down too heavily to sleep alone, had heard of my simple request. Her disapproval squared the shape of her body beneath her shawl and skirt.

Her wordlessness makes her valuable as a servant, as a vessel in my bed, yet there have been times, and this was one, when her unvoiced emotions erect a wall of guilt so thick I cower before it. I could not think what I had done to earn her disapproval. I thought I would never understand women even though I lived another fifty years.

They are the implacable arbiters of our behavior, demanding obedience to rules never broken, never thought of until, in the breaking of them, we are brought up short against the impenetrable barrier of female wrath.

I pushed my dish away. "Out with it," I said harshly, seeking dominance through bluster. "What've I done?"

She folded her arms across the boulders of her breasts, the proclaimer of destiny. Under their lids, her eyes were the edges of knives. "Not what you have done," she corrected. "What you intend."

"What?"

"You would disgrace that child," she said. "You would paint her. Dishonor her. Who would have her then? How could you think such a thing could be done?"

"Disgrace?" I said. "There's no disgrace. I wish to paint her. Do I disgrace the desert by painting it? Or the houses of the city? Where's the disgrace in that, eh?"

"Who will have her," she repeated, "after she has been here in your house? After you have taken her body and put it on your canvas for everyone to see? About you and me they say nothing. About you and this child they say . . . *how could you dare!*"

I slammed my fist on the table. The dishes jumped. The milk in the jug spilled over. I roared at her, taking refuge in the falseness of the accusation. "Her face! I wanted to paint her face, you fool!"

"So you say." She was quite calm. Male rage was as nothing to her. "But the face would not be enough, eh? The face is only a door to be opened."

"You're crazy." Pain struck me at the thought of what

107

I had loosed. I stood up. She looked at me, untouched by my emotions. "You didn't say that to her? You didn't tell that child I would paint her naked?"

The look in her eyes told me I was doomed. "Yes, I told her. She is almost a woman. She had to know."

I wanted to put my hands around the square golden column of her throat. I wanted her to pay—for my sin, for hers, for the deadly flower that is the world. I imagined it; the cutting edges of her eyes gone dull; her breasts running lifeless down her belly. I imagined for one moment only that I could obliterate the twining evils of religion, superstition, culture with a motion of my hands. I grabbed her.

As if outside myself, I saw the symbolism of the act, the ritual struggle. I saw the *paseo*, the game of widening circles played out in this valley, in a thousand valleys. I saw the children of the world doomed to capitulate to the cycle. I saw men like myself who believed they were free.

"Bitches!" I cried. "All of you! Evil, wicked bitches!" I let her go with such force that she fell against the table, hissing at me like a mountain cat.

I turned from her and ran, cutting across the plaza, scattering the little girls, the gentle sparrows. She was there, her eyes wide, her hands crossed over her breast like a shield.

I saw her but did not stop. Like the animal I am, I went to earth, back to the succor of the desert, where life exists in beauty and in barrenness and lays the bones of *penitentes* bare.

Simple Amy

Just about first light the phone rang. It was the police chief, with some far-fetched yarn about that preacher woman, Aimee Semple McPherson, who'd been missing out of California for a couple months. Seems she'd turned up in Agua Prieta just the other side of the line from Douglas, saying she'd been kidnapped.

"Ham," Percy says to me, his voice crackling like voices do over these country phone lines, "Ham, I want you to bring a couple of them hounds of yours down here quick as you can."

"How come?" I asked. "She's back, ain't she?"

"Yeah. But she's got this crazy story about a shack in Mexico where the kidnappers took her. If it's there, we got to know."

"Why?"

" 'Cause we do. We're dealin' with a famous person. Can't let whoever got her get away."

"They're probably long gone," I said. "My dogs won't find them."

"Don't give me that. We got to try, else I'll look like a fool in the next election."

Well, that much was true. "All right," I said, "but I bet you every person in Agua Prieta's been tromping all over and messed up the scent. And if she got kidnapped in California, what was she doing in Mexico?"

"Hell, I don't know! That's what we want to find out!"

"Give me an hour," I said, thinking how I'd been planning to spend the day doing not much of anything for a change.

"Hurry it up." The phone clicked.

I went out to the dog pens and was greeted like always—tails wagging, ears cocked as if to ask me what was up.

Lucy was a Blue Tick, with as good a nose on her as I ever came across. I called her and old Bell, who was older and steadier on the scent, not as likely to get distracted, and loaded them in the truck. Then I went back to the house and told Meggie where I was headed.

She opened her eyes so wide I thought they'd pop. "Her!" she said. "You mean she's *here?* How come she's here of all places?"

Meggie followed the news like a hound on the scent, and she'd been fascinated by the woman's disappearance, along with everybody else in the country. Except me. I never could trust a preacher, and especially not a woman preacher who acted more like she was in a melodrama than spreading the Lord's word. Something about the whole thing sounded.

"Makes no sense, at all," I said. "A woman like that."

"You don't know anything about a woman like that. Neither do I." She gave me a slap on the arm. "But make sure you remember everything so you can tell me."

"So you can tell the neighbors."

"Git!" She was laughing. She laughs a lot. Makes life a pleasure.

I got into town, and Perce took me over to the hospital

where the lady had been taken as a precaution. I needed something of hers so's Lucy and Bell would know what they were after.

Well, she was laying in that bed, all small and white and big-eyed, and the way she looked, the way her clothes looked, told me that, preacher or not, she was lying through her teeth. Why? Why does anybody lie? So's not to have to tell the truth.

There were her shoes, hardly worn, and I can tell you, if you walk a hundred yards in this country, your shoes are going to get scraped by stones, covered with dust, and muddy if you happen to get near a tank or a wash that's flowing. And if you've been living in a Mexican shack for a couple months, your clothes're going to look it and stink besides.

Out in the hall, I shook my head. "Perce," I said, "this here's a wild-goose chase. She's been holed up with some boyfriend, somewhere, and don't want to say. Maybe she got tired of the Lord and decided to come down to earth and have her a little fling without nobody knowing. That's her privilege, but we don't have to go along with it."

"Just in case she ain't lying, we got to go look. Hell, man, there's newspaper reporters all over town! I can't just go and make an accusation like that. Not about her. She's prob'ly the most famous woman in America."

"Are we going to have trouble with the *federales* over there?"

"Nope. They're in this with us. Everybody wants to make the papers."

111

I figured, if I was going to be news, I'd rather do it on my own. "Let's just get on with it," I said.

Well, it was just like I knew it would be. The street in front of the house where she'd gone to first had been tramped on by every cop, newsman, sightseer, and kid in creation, and the Mexicans was acting like it was a *fiesta*. I hadn't seen so much excitement since the match race between the American horse and a critter from Chihuahua.

Lucy gave me a look that said—"What kind of nonsense is this?"—and Bell just sat down and panted, his tongue hanging in the dust.

I said: "Perce, this ain't gonna work. If there was any chance at all of back trailing her, it was gone before you called me. This here's a circus, and we both know it."

He was holding the reins of two horses and tossed me a set. "Let's get started."

A posse had taken off shortly before. I could still see their dust far to the east. "You go after them," I told him. "Leave me and the dogs on our own."

He didn't like it. Maybe he was worried I'd come up with something and get the glory, but one thing he did have was common sense. "Meet me back at the office around four," he said.

I agreed just to get him moving. If my dogs struck any kind of a trail, I'd follow it to hell and back, and never mind the time of day or reporters and bigwigs from Los Angeles and the woman's million-dollar temple.

It was hot. The sky had that washed-out look it gets in early summer, and off in the distance the air shimmered and lifted in the heat. Even the mountains looked tired, like they was about to melt. The dogs and I swung to the south and west, not for any particular reason, or maybe because that's where the breeze was coming from, and I kept the horse at a slow jog right behind Lucy and Bell.

Almost right off, I found a cabin, an adobe so old it was running back into the ground, and most of the roof was gone, but I figured I'd take a look to be sure.

I swung down, tied the horse, and went inside with Lucy at my heels. She was growling deep in her throat, and that was all that kept me from stepping on the biggest rattlesnake I ever seen, thick as my wrist and sleeping off his dinner. Other than him and the rats, there hadn't anybody been in the place for fifty years.

That ugly critter coiled up—slowly—and I shot him. One less of the nasty things. And I cut off the rattles, twelve of them, for a souvenir of a day wasted.

When I got back outside, a rider on a big bay horse was headed toward me, probably because he'd heard my shot. I stood stark still, my hands in plain sight. Since the revolution, a man has to be careful where he goes or what he does down in Mexico, even this close to the line.

He came toward me at a walk, and after a minute I recognized Hector Cisneros. I was on his land, and a few years back I'd bought some weaner calves from him—after my dogs had found the lion that had been living off his herd.

"*Hola*, Ham. *¿Que tal?*" He pulled up, a grin and his

113

question on a face that always reminded me of a pirate's.

I told him, and he listened, puzzled. "A woman? There's been no woman here. I would have known it."

That was true. Hector knew every stone and cave on his place. If there had been kidnappers, living in a shack anywhere on his thousands of acres, he or his *vaqueros* would have found them.

"Go home," he said. "It's too hot to be chasing smoke."

"Why'd she lie?"

He shrugged. "Perhaps like Juan the Baptist, she went out in the desert to talk to God. Or perhaps she go off with a lover. Who can say?"

"It's damned peculiar, you ask me."

"To us," he said. "Not to her. And what man ever understood the mind of a woman?"

He was right, I guessed. Even Meggie wouldn't be able to explain this one, for all she listened to Amy preach over the radio and was fascinated by her disappearance. Meggie was a no-nonsense woman and dead honest. In all the years we'd been married, she'd never looked at another man, never told a lie, at least not that I knew. She and I were a pair, two peas in a pod, and I was glad of it. The two of us made sense out of the world, more sense than I'd ever heard out of the mouth of any preacher. Thinking about her made me wish I was back home.

Lucy and Bell came at a lope when I called, glad to quit what was plainly useless, and they headed for the border, tails high.

"If you find anything, let me or Percy know," I said to Hector.

He showed his teeth in a smile. "There will be nothing, *amigo*. She and her angels have hidden her tracks too well. *Adiós*."

All this fuss over one little woman. If Calvin Coolidge himself had disappeared, there wouldn't have been such a ruckus. But as it was, Douglas had its day, made headlines in all the papers, and the Gadsden Hotel was bursting with newsmen and folks who just came out of curiosity like some go to freak shows. McPherson's mother come in on the train, along with her kids who were all dressed up and looked kind of scared, like they didn't know whether to laugh or cry.

Then, as if there wasn't enough of a ruckus, the town big shots decided to have a parade and a picnic in the woman's honor. When Meggie heard about it, nothing could keep her home.

"I want to see for myself," she said. "I want to know."

"Know what?"

"How she does it."

"Does what?"

She made a face at me like I was slow-witted. "Gets everybody to do what she wants."

"I bet she won't tell you."

"Probably not, but still. . . ." Her voice faded out and left me to wonder.

"Don't I do what you want?" I asked then.

"Most times." She gave a little laugh like she was embarrassed, then her face wrinkled up. "It's just . . .

I'm curious. There's things I don't know about. There's women like her making their way in the world, and then there's me and my neighbors, and we don't do much except what's needed. Maybe there's more to livin' than that."

I might have got mad, but she was serious. "You and me's got a good life," I said.

"That's not what I meant." She looked down at her feet, and then up at me. "It's not anything I ever tried to say. It just come to mind all of a sudden. But we're going to that picnic, Ham Bartlett, or you'll never hear the end of it!"

Of course, we went, stood there on G Avenue, watched the parade, and hollered like everybody else as the woman rode past, waving, a smile on her face.

People came from all over—from Rodeo, Portal, Lordsburg, and Tombstone, even the Lee boys from Paradise, who had a really famous pack of lion dogs, hunted them as far away as South America. Later I heard they named the lion their dogs couldn't catch, Simple Amy, after the heroine of the year.

At the Tenth Street Park they had tents and awnings set up, and tables loaded with more food than I thought anybody could eat. Kids were running everywhere, and a band was playing from the bandstand. I was standing there, just taking it all in, when Meggie grabbed my arm. "Here she comes!"

The band stopped playing, and everybody stood up and got quiet.

"Why, she's just a little mite of a thing," Meggie said,

surprised, I guess, that so much trouble could come out of such a small package.

The woman climbed the steps to the bandstand, slowly, then turned and reached out her arms like she wanted to pull all of us closer. Everybody cheered, and then got quiet again when she started to praise the Lord for bringing her back from the fire of the desert. Washed clean of sin, she was, just like all the rest of us would be.

Let me tell you, she had a kind of magic in her. It stopped you in your tracks and made you listen whether you wanted to or not. Right then I thought she was two people, and each had convinced the other that whatever they did was right. Only trouble was, she hadn't convinced me. She was a little actress, and she was layin' it on.

When she was finished, I wandered off, saw Viola Slaughter who loved her parties as well as the next, sitting under an awning. She'd been living in town since just before old John died, and I figured she'd surely have something to say about the goings on.

She and John had been friends of my dad's and of Meggie and me for a long time, and she was still as pretty as the days when she first courted old John and married him.

"Howdy, Viola," I said, and she looked up at me out of those big eyes of hers.

"Ham. It's been a while. The ranch must be keeping you busy."

"Not near as busy as all this funny business."

She laughed. "I hear they're still out searching for that shack."

"Good luck to them."

"You don't believe her?"

"Do you?"

She sipped her lemonade and smiled. "I think she's got a secret. All women do, you know."

The way she said it, the twinkle in her eye, made me think she had her own share of secrets that she'd never told and never would, that even John hadn't known all that went on in that head of hers. Made me wonder if Meggie had things she'd kept hidden from me all those years. The notion of that made me feel out of balance, like I was walking a tightrope over a cañon, and one move the wrong direction would do me in.

Viola reached out and took my arm. "Don't look so stunned. Secrets aren't the end of the world. Come on, let's go find Meggie."

Later I saw the two of them laughing together, and wondered if women told each other things they never told their men. I wondered if wives didn't have something like a club where they whispered about their husbands, talked about stuff that didn't have no place in real life, something like Meggie had tried to tell me.

For a minute or two I was sad, like there was an empty space inside where before there had been contentment. Then Meggie saw me and waved.

"Where've you been? I've been looking all over for you. Have you ever seen such a mob?"

She smelled like soap and rose water, like Meggie,

and the loneliness I'd felt was gone, just like that. "Well," I said, "did you find out what you wanted?"

Her answer wasn't what I expected, though I'm not sure just what I did expect, given the thoughts I'd been having. She said: "That's not a happy woman."

"Who?"

"Her." She gestured with her chin to where McPherson was standing with her children. "She wants attention so bad, she's willing to make a fool of herself and the rest of us to get it."

"I dunno," I said. "I just figured she was hiding something."

Meggie put her arm through mine. "Guess we'll never know. I reckon if she's got a secret, it's between her and the Lord."

There was that word again. "What's all this?" I asked because I just had to. "First Viola, and then you, making out like everybody's not telling the truth. Are you keepin' secrets from me?" I said it, and then waited, still balanced on that high wire.

What she did, my Meggie, was giggle that laugh of hers that sounds like bubbling water, and she looked up at me out of her blue eyes as flirty as when we was courting.

"That's for me to know, and you to find out," she said, tugging on my arm. "Now come on, Ham. Let's go home."

China Doll

From where I sit behind the curtain, I watch the white demons—the men with hairy faces and hungry eyes, carrying pistols, the women who rush along the street on big, ugly feet but who, at least, have the freedom to walk out, to talk to one another, to be seen without disgrace.

You must understand that my husband, to whom I was married when I was fifteen, is a good man. I do not raise my voice in anger to him or whine because, even here, he follows the old ways and keeps me in this house so no one can look upon my face.

He is afraid that another man might think me beautiful and steal me, or take advantage of the fact that I am Chinese and without protection in this town with the bad luck name. Tombstone.

I have spent many hours looking at my face in the mirror, and what looks back at me is a face like any other so that I ask, if it is beautiful, how is that my fault? To everyone beauty appears as they wish it. What the eye sees is not always what is there. I know this. I have had many months to think about such things, to watch the life that passes outside my window, to wish I might someday go out, perhaps even as far as the mountains.

They rise up out of the desert like great stone walls, the frozen waves of an ancient sea. On the mountains, I think, there must be silence with only the wind music, like a flute, and perhaps the scent of flowers that bloom in secret places.

When the rain comes, it brings with it a sweetness, the scents of herbs and spices and old fires, and it is then that I wish to go out, feel it on my face, taste it on my tongue, and laugh as I did as a child.

Here in town is always the noise of a thousand people, a smell not even storm can wash away—wood smoke, animals and their droppings, and the dust that rises off the street, the indigestible food of the white demons and how it inhabits their clothes, their skin, so that even my husband complains of it.

These people have come here in search of the silver that lies under the ground, and all day, all night the men burrow like rats into the heart of earth, hoping to find riches and never seeing the ugliness that they have created in their obsession. From the brothels and saloons come the sounds of music and harsh laughter, and gunshots keep me awake in the bed where my husband lies, snoring, beside me.

I hear him now, moving around in the store where he sells all that anyone might need, even the opium for the dens beneath the streets where white men and Chinese alike go to pursue their dreams.

On the nights when my husband, too, goes out for the evening to gamble, smoke, enjoy the visions that come, I go into the store and admire the porcelains, the watermelon seeds and salted plums, the cigars and tobacco, the carved ivory and jade, and the containers of precious tea, the hidden casks of opium.

It is a room of treasures, this shop of my husband's, and, as I go about by lamp light, the scents of anise and incense and chrysanthemum flowers make my head whirl as if I, too, have smoked the forbidden drug and walk in a mist.

Last night the woman came and rattled the door and called out as if demons were at her heels and she could feel the heat of their breath through her clothes. She called for my husband in a voice as hoarse as the scratching of the cicadas that we used to catch and keep in cages.

"Sam Wong! Sam Wong!"

I whispered through the door. "He not here."

"Let me in!" There was despair in the voice, a plea I could not ignore.

I opened the door and saw a white woman with wild eyes and hair the color of a red bridal gown. "Not here!" I repeated. "You go now."

"Where is he?"

I shook my head.

"Damned dumb Chinese," she said with an explosion behind her eyes.

I went to shut her out, but she grabbed my wrist. "Where's he keep it? You know."

She had big hands, and I pulled back, afraid, not for myself but for the child in my belly that had begun to grow. Fear gave me courage. I pushed my face close to hers, close to the stink and the madness, and hissed at her like a snake. "You get out. You go Mary Sing-choy for opium or I call police."

She let go and laughed. "That's a funny one. He might even believe you."

I recognized her then. She was the wife of the policeman, the one named Earp. I wondered if he knew she was wandering the streets of Hoptown, pounding on doors, looking for a drug to pleasure herself? From him she received no pleasure. I had seen him with another, a woman any man would take as concubine. Even in the fancy houses of Canton, which, of course, I have never seen, that woman would be called beautiful.

I had no words to tell this white ghost the sorrow I felt. Even in my own language there is no proper way to tell a woman that her husband no longer desires her.

I stepped inside and stood trembling, for the first time glad that my husband thinks I am a treasure to be locked up. Better this than be set free to walk the streets, begging for attention, for opium to dull the pain in the heart.

Mei-Ling, the servant girl that my husband found through Mary Sing-choy—called China Mary by everyone, here, and who rules over Hoptown with a power unusual in a woman—comes in from the market with a chicken and a basket of fresh vegetables. As always, I ask her what she has seen, what is for sale in the market. I have watched the Mexicans, leading mules and donkeys burdened with pots and pans, striped blankets, crates of chickens and ducks, strings of red peppers and garlic that remind me of home, and cages of small birds that must sing though I can't hear them. What I want, more than money, more than pearls is one of those bright birds to keep me company, to sing while I sit looking out or embroidering the slippers we all wear inside the house.

Mei-Ling has already killed the chicken. Its head hangs limp, its beak open as if in protest.

"Go back," I tell her. "Go back and buy me a song-bird for the house."

She stares at me, her mouth hanging open like the chicken's so I can see her brown teeth. She is stupid, and her feet are unbound and hideous in their straw san-dals, but she does well enough as a servant.

"Why are you standing there?" I ask. "Go and do as I say. Bring me a bird. A pretty one that sings."

When my husband comes in for dinner, the bird is in its cage beside the window. "What jewel is this?" he asks, peering at the brilliant green, blue, and yellow feathers.

"It doesn't sing." I have spent the day trying to break its silence.

"It is enough that it is beautiful." He makes his pro-nouncement, then goes to the table and waits to be served the meal.

We eat without speaking. I turn his words around in my head, looking for an answer, but can find no answer. How, after all, can I argue with him about beauty or anything at all? I have not been taught to express the thoughts that spin in my head. I have been taught accep-tance and how to please, to do so quietly without dis-ruption. I swallow my tears with the rice, and smile.

The child beats on my belly as if it is a drum. "Patience," I say to him. "Be patient. You have months yet. And when you have been in the world one hundred days, I will have your future told. May it be far from here, and I with you."

The bird croaks. Mei-Ling says it is called a parrot and can be taught to speak. Every day I talk to it, but perhaps it cannot understand my language, for it only makes strange sounds that mean nothing. He and I sit by the window, looking out. The weather is cold now, the sky over the mountains pale blue, and dark clouds fly quickly past like large birds of bad fortune. They make me afraid. Of what I don't know.

On the street the women clutch shawls around them, and the wind blows their skirts. Several times I have seen the woman with the red hair, her face a mask of tragedy. She seems to have grown older like a plant that is not watered and droops on a weakened stem.

I have seen the other woman, too, the woman with a face like a white lily. She clutches the arm of the policeman as if she is afraid he will disappear before her eyes, and I wonder how it will turn out, this love affair I read from a distance, this play without words.

Where is beauty now? How is this gourd that is my body enticing? I have grown so large my feet won't support me, and I cannot walk without help.

But my husband is pleased. He has been to the fortune-teller who told him I will bear him a son, so he brings me gifts—flower-scented teas, a necklace of green jade, a painting of plum blossoms that I have hung on the wall where I can see it from my chair, taste the gentleness of spring like the bees in the hearts of flowers that hum with happiness. And still my bird neither sings nor speaks.

Two sons! I have two sons! My husband struts like a peacock as if he has done it all, while I look at the perfection of two small faces and feel I will crack open with joy.

How quickly pain is forgotten! I do not remember the hours of the births. A blessing. What I remember is the sound of gunshots just before the pain began, and people crowding the street, men and women rushing like ants to honey.

"What's happening? Go and find out!" I ordered Mei-Ling, who went in a hurry, waddling on those splayed feet.

"The white policeman who looks like a tiger has killed three men," she reported when she returned.

"A tiger?" There are times when Mei-Ling sees what others don't.

She nodded. "One who will kill again, many times. Now he has the taste for it in his mouth."

"Ah."

I had no time to wonder about him or his future, for the next moment the pain began, and for a day and a night nothing existed but my body breaking apart.

We celebrate the days before the New Year with offerings of rice dumplings to the Kitchen God. Ming and Pao, my sons, lie in the *amah*'s arms and watch as the incense carries our prayers to heaven.

Now there are three women and two babies in my house, and it is not as lonely as before, but I wish with all my heart to be in China where I should go and pay my respects to my parents and my husband's parents for the New Year. I wish for my sons to know and love their ancestors as is proper.

Once I whispered to my husband of my desire, but he said only that the babies were too small to think about such a trip—across the desert, across the ocean with its storms and waves that can sink even the best ships.

Still, I will bring it up again—and again—until he agrees. I miss my father's house with its two courtyards and the pool where the carp quiver and flash, where the children play, filling the air with their silver laughter. I miss the friendship of women like myself, their complaints, their games, the sometimes frivolous but always comforting conversations.

While I pray to the Kitchen God, the white men shoot at each other. Mei-Ling tells me that the brother of the policeman was shot. He will not die, but I wonder what the Earp tiger will do? I wonder if his concubine is happy with him who walks his own way.

Mary Sing-choy sits, drinking tea and eating the peanuts and salted plums I have set out on the small table. She is a large woman and dignified, one who understands the ways of power. She owns the contracts of every Chinese who comes here, legal or not, and her opium parlor is always filled with those who go to lose themselves in visions.

She watches me over the edge of the teacup, and her eyes sparkle with a wicked humor as if she knows a joke I haven't heard and might not understand.

She has come with presents for Ming and Pao, and for a long time she held them both on her lap, speaking nonsense. If she hadn't done this, I would be afraid of her—her size, her air of command.

"So," she says, putting down the cup and folding her hands, "you wish to go home."

The statement startles me. "How do you know?"

"Your husband. He worries that you might become ill with wishing."

My husband carries worries on his shoulders like water buckets, but I don't say that. I only smile.

"Well?" One plucked eyebrow makes a wing on her forehead.

I begin slowly, searching for a way to speak that does not sound like a complaint. "My husband honors me," I say at last. "And for that I am thankful. But like the bird, I am a prisoner here in this town, this house. And my children . . . I worry they will grow up as foreigners with no country, no home at all. It is a bad thing not to belong to a place, to be always searching for something left behind."

She sighs and rearranges the folds of her robe. The jewels on her fingers shine, and the scent of sandal-

128

wood is strong, somehow comforting as I wait for her answer.

"Many times," she says after a minute, "many times I have thought there is a curse on this town. After all, what can be expected from a place named for a grave?" Again her eyes glint with malice. "These white men are very stupid, not so different from our own bandits except that they respect nothing. Not the past, not their god, not even themselves. I've watched them just as you have, from behind your curtain, and I know this. Still, I have made a life here better than I could imagine, and, when I die, my bones will go back to China for burial. For me that's enough. For you . . . you are sick in your heart with wanting. So . . . I will speak to your husband and make it right with him."

She pushes up from her chair. "Now come with me to the door."

Alive with happiness, I stutter out my poor thanks, but she silences me with a wave of her hand. "You have your sons. Take care of them. Teach them honor and love for their family and their ancestors."

"I will," I say, and mean it. "I will, Mary Sing-choy."

"And when you've seen me out, let your bird go free." Her expression is unreadable, but her meaning is clear.

I bow my head in obedience, and so she will not see the tears that have come to my eyes.

I am like the bird that refused to leave its cage and had to be lured to the windowsill with crumbs of rice cake.

Even then it hesitated, afraid to try its wings.

"Go!" I commanded, pushing the bird with my hand. "Go where you belong!"

After a long time it flew, a painted arrow, toward the mountains that I have never walked on, only touched with my eyes.

At Mary Sing-choy's urging, my husband at last granted me permission to return to China, accompanied by Mei-Ling and the *amah*, both sworn to protect me with their lives. In San Francisco we will be met by my cousin, who will act as my guardian on the long sea voyage.

I do not know whether to sing with joy or to weep at leaving my husband who will follow when he has saved enough money to secure our future life. I wonder if it is safe to leave him behind, where the white demons kill for their own twisted reasons, and their women walk the streets in fear and sorrow. I wonder if he might take a second wife who will replace me in his heart. So, you see how much I resemble the bird that could not make up its mind even when given what it wanted.

"You will come?" I ask my husband as he holds me so close I am aware of his body beneath his clothes.

"Soon," he whispers.

For a long time he looks at my face, then pulls down the veil, and I am hidden from him and the eyes of others. I press my lips together, suppressing anger, knowing that as soon as I leave him I will tear it away and let the sun kiss me.

We make a happy procession on our way to the stagecoach that will take us to the train, the railroad built with the picks and shovels, the sweat of my own people. Mary Sing-choy lifts Pao high in her arms, and Ah Lum carries Ming whose laughter winds around us like tiny bells. Behind them come well-wishers and servants, carrying the trunks.

A wind whirls dust down the street. When the little cyclone has passed I see wagons and a coffin, and the woman with her red hair, hidden now by a black bonnet. She holds the arm of another, prettier woman who weeps and cannot stop. The tiger is with them, his eyes like agates seen underwater, his mouth a straight line carved from stone.

I turn away from their grief and from the rage in him that reaches out like cold fire and surrounds us all. "What has happened?" I ask in a whisper.

"The brother of the policemen has been murdered." My husband's hand is tight on my arm. "Do not look at them. They are all cursed."

"Where are they going?"

"To California for the burial."

Death will be on the train with me. "No!" The word comes out small because suddenly I am nothing—a grain of sand, a bird moved by the wind of ill fortune.

Mary Sing-choy places Pao in my arms. "Life and death run parallel. You can't avoid death, but this day you go with life. The dead man can't harm you."

"But the tiger will have revenge."

For a minute she seems puzzled, then she nods. "Wyatt Earp is a man, and angry. He'll fight, and his

131

women will stay home and pray. But don't worry. His destiny isn't yours."

What will I remember when I am home and safe behind familiar walls? The town sprouting like a fungus in darkness and blotting out beauty? Mountains of rock that shine pink in the dawn? The lace of strange trees beside a river I never used as mirror?

Will I replay the soundless play I watched, writing my own words in place of the actual, moving the actors on the dusty street—the woman with the terrible face, the concubine as graceful as a flower but not present with the mourners on this day, or the tiger with his fury coiled within?

Their procession moves off ahead, moving slowly and surrounded by riders who carry rifles and who watch the road with sharp and terrible eyes. The tiger sits his tall horse as a warrior should, and for the first time I understand the feelings of the concubine, who loves him for his courage. Where has he hidden her, I wonder. What fears are hers?

After awhile our coach, too, is in motion, going so fast I can do no more than wave good bye. My breath catches in my throat, and for a moment I cannot breathe. The little house, my husband, the wife that I was all lay behind, hidden in the dust. Who am I now?

I give my sons over to the *amah*, lean out the window and rip the veil from my face. It is as I imagined. The sun dazzles. The shadows are gone.

Sunflower

No one seeing Clay and me now—Clay, sitting on the rusted chair under the live oak, the spectacles he got at the dime store slipping down his nose because, whatever he says, I know he's taking a nap and not reading the Bible, and me, gone gray-headed like the seed pod of a sunflower and small-breasted to boot—no one would think I was young once and so foolish I near ruined my marriage and myself.

They mightn't even think I paid the price for what I did, seeing Clay and me contented, in a decent house, curtains at the windows, my flowers and my yellow cat by the door.

They'd be wrong, though. The Bible tells us—"As ye sow, so shall ye reap."—and it's true. Not that life's been all bad or all that hard to take, but I figure there could have been a bit more joy in it, the kind of lightweight feeling I used to have, just fit to bursting with excitement and romance. The way I felt when I was young and yellow-haired, and every man for fifty miles was courting me, lining up on the front porch, evenings, or crowding around to dance on a Saturday night at the fairgrounds, and stealing a kiss or two in the shadows by the corrals.

Maybe, though, feelings like that belong only to the young, have no place when you're sobered up and married. I don't know. I never spoke about it to anyone, not even Clay, never to Clay. He's been good to me, better

133

than I deserve, but I never felt I could ask him where the joy went, the mystery, the never knowing what's going to happen, only that it's going to be so wonderful you're not sure you can stand it. He might have thrown it up to me, and I don't think I could've stood that.

I used to wake up happy every morning back then, and run to the window to see what kind of day it promised to be, and then to the old mirror where I'd stand and brush my hair and shake it loose like silk. Then back to the window to see if Miguel had left his scarf tied around the corral post. If he had, it meant I'd find him somewhere, and we'd go off, not for long because he was supposed to be working. But we'd find time for kisses down by the wash, and we'd talk a bit, and, later on, we got more serious, touching, lying together under an old tree whose branches came down all the way to the ground and made a kind of tent.

My ma and pa never knew about those meetings. Or my sisters or brothers, either. No one ever found out, even after I married Clay, after I knew I'd made a mistake and tried to change it.

It was just that I was young and didn't know much about folks or about love, either. What Miguel and I did down by the wash had nothing to do with living. It had nothing to do with the way my parents acted together, or with the way any grown folks acted, all tight and tired and full of dos and don'ts.

What we did was wild and sweet as the flowers we crushed under us, as the branches moved overhead, and now and again a bird singing as if we weren't even there, or as if we belonged. What we did didn't need words, though Miguel had plenty in two languages, and he called me every pretty name he knew and made promises I believed in. We'd have us a ranch someday, over the border in Mexico, and we'd be rich, and I'd wear ruffled dresses, and all the men would tremble at the sight of my yellow hair, my blue eyes, my breasts firm and ripe as apples. I'd lie there with my arms around him, my face in his hair, believing it all.

One day though, my pa called me in and told me to choose. Just that. "Choose," he said, "and let the county go on about its business." And clear the way for my young sisters rearing at my heels.

I swear I never thought choosing would end it. I don't know why. I guess I was just plain dumb. Dream-struck. I thought life would go on easy, and me sucking the sweetness out like a bee.

So I chose. I looked them over, all those men, rich and poor, smart and some dumber even than I was, and I thought of Clay Eddy who didn't come around much but who had a way of looking at me out of his gray eyes that made me shiver when I remembered it. Clay who never talked much, but who told me once I had a laugh like water in a creek, and, if he had a thirst, he'd walk ten miles to get to me.

The Eddys were a big family and well-off. There's been Eddys here since the early days, always will be. But none of ours. Not even a yellow-haired daughter from the two of us. We were mismatched from the start.

Clay's father gave us a section up in the foothills as a

wedding present, and Clay, well, he was set on moving there as soon as possible. "We got to have our own place," he kept saying. "Our own place" those first months was a lean-to out in a pasture. We were ten miles from our neighbors and years away from town, from laughter, dancing, and Miguel.

I was a married woman off in the high country with a man I didn't really know. A man who was mainly silent and thinking, who didn't dance and had no time for company. He was building "our own place." I cooked over an open fire in that lean-to, and bedded down at night on an old mattress he'd drug up in the wagon, and I remembered how Miguel and I had lain in the grass and laughed and touched and never worried if we knew each other or not.

Sometimes at night, Clay would sit out front, looking at the stars and naming them. He'd say—"Come out and sit, Susannah."—and I'd go out for a spell, and he'd tell me about the stars and the planets, about things I didn't understand and didn't care about. I wanted to dance. I wanted to go down on a Saturday night and be twirled around by my husband, followed by the men I'd spurned, envied by the girls. I wanted Clay to tell me about my laugh, about my hair, about how he was building a ranch to make us rich to buy me things. All he ever talked about those nights was stars and history.

I felt like the girl I was had died and been resurrected into a woman I didn't recognize and couldn't get the shape of. Worse, that seemed to be what everyone expected. No one thought it was hard on me, going off with my husband. They made jokes and laughed and teased, and told me how lucky I was and how clever to have married an Eddy, to have caught Clay, the hardest working of them all.

I guess that saved him though. When I disappointed him, he threw himself into whatever he was doing to forget. I disappointed him from the start. I could never be easy with him, not in talk or in bed. A man has rights once he's married. I knew that. But I couldn't relax with him, and after a while he took to watching me as if he expected to find out something, as if he were puzzled and looking for an answer.

"I wish you'd quit watching me," I said one day.

He blew out smoke from his cigarette and stared at me. "I never heard it was wrong, takin' pleasure lookin' at your wife," he said.

"It just makes me jumpy. Like I did wrong."

"Did you?"

I turned on him quick as a deer. "No!" I shouted. "No."

"Well, then," he said, "you got no reason to worry."

He went outside to watch his stars and didn't come in till after I'd gone to bed. He didn't wake me like he did sometimes, calling "Suze," low in my ear, his hand on my breast. Not that night or the next.

But then he came in carrying the biggest bunch of wildflowers I ever saw. He knew I loved flowers, and he stuck them in a jug on the table and said he'd been thinking we should take the wagon and go see my folks and then stop a while in town.

I thought of Miguel, and hugged Clay tight around his waist. He closed his eyes and said—"Suze, Suze...."— and took his way with me right there.

By September, we had two rooms built and roofed over with tin. There was space to expand "when the time comes," Clay said. He was thinking of sons. Everyone was, even my folks and his. Everyone but me. I kept thinking about winter. About being snowed in and no way out and nothing to do but sew on the new machine Clay bought me, or look out at the junipers covered up, bent down with ice. Every time I thought about it, I'd panic like an animal in a trap because I had no place else to go.

When I said I'd like to spend a month down in the valley, Clay looked at me. His eyes had shadows in them as if I'd hit him and it hurt, but all he said was: "You'll like it up here, Suze. Give it a chance. You've never seen these mountains in the snow. Or listened to 'em." One side of his mouth curved up. "You got to learn to be easy. To take what comes and go with it. Stop fighting the bridle."

"And you got to stop talking to me like I'm one of your horses," I said. "I don't like it here, all quiet with nothing to do but work in the garden or pedal that machine. No people, no fun, no nothing day in and day out. Why should I sew anyhow? Who ever sees me?"

"I'm here," he said. "Or don't I count?"

It went on like that, peaceable for days, and then we'd start cutting at each other with sharp little words, and then with no words at all until I thought I'd scream just to smash the quiet.

I spent weeks canning vegetables, filling the shelves with food for the winter, putting down pork in brine, and curing bacon. I did it all because I'd been raised to it, not because I was proud, or set a good table, or wanted to please. I did it because it was harvest, and because, if I hadn't, I'd have gone mad.

In September, Clay went off on a roundup and left me alone. I cried, walked the floor, chewed down my fingernails till they bled, and I thought of taking the mule and running off, but, as I said, I had no place to go. My folks would've sent me back as fast as I'd gone.

Then, toward sunset one evening, Miguel came up on his big paint horse. He knew Clay was gone, and he took the chance. When I saw him, I bawled like a calf and brought him inside and learned what it was I'd given away so easy. What I could never get back.

That winter, war was declared. There was fighting in places I'd never heard of and couldn't imagine. Clay bought us a radio, ran it off batteries he powered with the windmill. We didn't have electric here till years later—we're that isolated. All winter I sat and listened to that radio—music mostly, and the love stories, and, when Clay wasn't around, I sang some and danced and made believe Miguel was there with me. Because Clay, when he came in, he had to have the news, had to get his old books off the shelf and look up all those places with their funny names. He'd get to talking about wars and generals, armies and back history till I thought I'd scream.

One night I did scream, I was just so tired of hearing about the Japanese and the Germans. "Whyn't you go enlist, you're so fascinated?" I yelled.

"You'd dance plenty, then," he said. "I can see it all. You making fools of us both." He clicked off the radio, put his books back neat the way he did everything.

"Come spring, you go down to your folks," he said. "I've signed on as foreman at Howson's. We're going to be busy selling beeves to the Army. Maybe when I'm done, you'll have growed up a bit."

After that, he slept in the barn with Ringer, the mule. I remember hoping he'd freeze in there. I remember thinking he cared more for that mule than for me, and I didn't know whether to be glad of it or cry.

So I went home and found everybody too busy to worry about whether I was happy or not. It was spring, the prettiest time. The cactus was blooming, and the yuccas were in bud, and the washes were all running with the thaw. Everywhere I looked, I saw critters making nests or giving birth. Even my own sister who'd caught a husband right after me was swelling up with child.

I started meeting Miguel under the tree, going back to dreaming like I'd never left. I was Susannah again, and I had a dark, quick-fingered man who loved me, called me his angel, put the magic back in me.

But nothing ever lasts. Not happiness anyway. Not that feeling like you're all in one piece and proud of it. I was like a cactus that blooms for a night, throws all its sweetness into a tiny space, and then withers on the stem.

The Army caught up with Miguel. He couldn't prove he had any need to stay where he was, not with ten other cowboys to do his job. Besides, he was Mexican. Nobody cares about them. I was the only one, and his mother down on the border with a bunch of other children.

I cared so much I went off to town the day before he left. We took a room in the hotel where the salesmen stay, and the cattle buyers. We had one night, using the bed for what it was made for, over and over, and me crying like a young 'un and holding on like I was fighting off the whole U.S. government and the President to boot.

I went to the station, too. I hurt so bad I didn't care who saw me, who would go running to Clay with the news. I couldn't imagine any life after I watched that train ease out through the mesquite and the scrub toward the mountains and the sea.

I stood there a long time, till I couldn't see anything but its smoke, and, when I turned around, it was like I wasn't anybody at all. I never saw the man till I walked right into him, and then what I saw was the watch chain across his stomach. Even today, all I remember about him is that watch chain and his eyes, flat like dimes and colorless, with nothing behind them so he looked blind.

"Whoa there, miss," he said. "Everything all right?"

"No," I said, backing off, trying to go around him.

He figured it out pretty quick. "Your boyfriend, huh?

Too bad. Too bad." Those window glass eyes of his flashed at me.

"Leave me be," I said. "Just leave me be."

"That's just what I won't do," he said. "You go walking out on the street like that, you'll get killed. I'll walk along with you." He took my arm and somehow moved me out to the street.

"Now," he said, "you got some place to go?"

I had never had any place to go. I shook my head.

"Now look, miss," he said. "You got someone waiting? You can't just stand here in the street."

"The hotel," I said. "I'll get there."

"You will, and that's a fact because that's where I'm going." He started walking fast, his hand under my elbow.

I didn't say anything. There didn't seem to be words to get rid of him. I didn't protest either when he steered me into the hotel bar. It was dark in there and cool. I leaned my head back against the leather seat.

"You need a drink," he said. "What'll you have?"

I said: "Lemonade."

That made him laugh. I remember that—him laughing so hard people turned to look.

He brought me a glass that had ice in it, and a red cherry, and a slice of orange.

"You drink that," he said. "That's more like it."

I did, tasting it carefully first, like a horse testing water. It was good, that drink. I gulped it down, sweet and sour and cold, and ate the orange and the cherry.

He brought me another. After a while even those wall

eyes of his didn't bother me, or the fact that, under the table, his hand moved up my leg clear to the top.

Nothing seemed to matter. Looking back, I sometimes wonder what does matter. Whether what people do on this earth makes a speck of difference. If I'd just settled down in the mountains with Clay and never gone off to that hotel, would that have made my days different? Or Clay's? I somehow doubt it. People throw their time of grace away, one way or another, without stopping to think that maybe that's the happiest they'll ever be.

Mornings, now, I don't get up and run to the window or look in the mirror. Certainly there's nothing I'll see in the glass will make me feel better. Scrawny, with a gap in my side teeth where the wall-eyed man hit me. The other places don't show. I'm the only one knows they're there except Clay, and he's been trying to forget as long as I have.

I don't remember all of what happened. Don't want to. He got me drunk. Me, the dumb girl from the mountain who'd never tasted hard liquor in her life and didn't know what it could do taken on top of grief and a sleepless night.

He got me upstairs to that little room I'd been in with Miguel. When he started pulling at me, I fought back, I remember that much. That's when he hit me, hard, across the face so my teeth cracked and my nose started to bleed.

He called me names, too, and said some awful words, and I tried to scream. He held me down on the floor, one big hand across my throat so I could hardly breathe. I spattered blood across his shirt front where that watch chain was. That's what I saw. That and those weird flat eyes like stones, and the man part of him pushing out of his trousers, ugly and red and made for hurting, for coming at me until something cracked in my head, and I couldn't feel or see anything at all.

Thing is, nobody knew who he was, and I was in no shape to give any description. I lay on that floor till the next day when the girl came in to make the bed and found me. Then I lay in the hospital like I was dead for a week. Every time I woke up, I'd start screaming, so they had to give me things to keep me asleep. I remember my ma's face, her mouth in a straight line like it used to get when she was mad, and her eyes all red like she'd been crying. Clay was there, too, in his city suit, sitting beside the bed. I started screaming when I saw him. I was afraid he'd come at me with those cold words of his, afraid of what he'd say, what he'd call me. The wall-eyed man's words were still loud in my head.

But Clay was always there. Whenever I'd open my eyes, I'd see him, hands between his knees, edgy, the way he gets when he's in the house too long.

Finally I said: "Don't you have anything to do but sit there watching me?" It was horrible to say that, and him faithful as a hound all that time, but I figured I'd get it over with.

He said: "You feel better?"

"No," I said.

"Your ma's been in every day. She's staying at your Aunt Fran's."

"Where've you been?"

"Here," he said.

I thought about that. I couldn't fathom it, him staying there with me. "What for?" I asked.

"I had to see you were all right."

I started to cry. "All right," I said. "I'll never be all right. And you got no reason to stay here. Not now."

"You're my wife, Suze," he said. "Don't you know what that means?"

I didn't. I never had. Truth was, I'd never thought about much besides myself.

"You can divorce me. You got reason," I said.

He bent over the bed and looked at me. I think I'll always remember how he took a piece of my hair and looked at it like he'd never seen it before.

"What happened was a fool thing," he said finally. "And I'm not blaming you. Maybe it's part my fault, too, for leaving you alone." He spread my hair out over his hand. "I came to take you home, but maybe that's a fool thing, too. I thought I'd get you well, up on the mountain, but you can't stand it there, can you? Not the place. Not me."

I'd stood him well enough before we were married. I thought about that. About the silence between us, high as a wall.

"You used to talk so pretty," I said. "Now you just talk about things I don't care about. Things I don't understand. Then you come at me like you don't care, just because you got the right."

His mouth slanted up on one side in that way he has of laughing at the world. "I care," he said, "but a man can't change his nature."

"And I can't change mine."

"Is that it, then?" he asked.

I didn't know. I hurt, inside and out. I had nowhere to go, no one except him to care for me, and every thought I had and tried to follow whirled away like flood water, muddy and quick. The thing was, I didn't have any other life. I'd been a daughter, then a wife, with only a few hours of something else between. Something that glittered and was gone, fool's gold, mirage. But Clay was there, steady as those stars of his. "I care," he'd said.

"I'll come home." I closed my eyes so I wouldn't see the brightness on his face. It was something that didn't rightfully belong to me.

He put his hands on my shoulders easy, and then around my face. "If you don't like it there, we can go some place else."

He was too close. I needed a longer time. I kept my eyes closed. "It'll do fine," I said.

A week later, we went home.

Miguel got killed in the second year of the war on an island in an ocean I've never seen but have to believe is there because everyone says it is.

And Clay and I have just stayed here on the mountain, doing like folks have always done, working to feed ourselves and put a little by.

Clay put in a flower garden for me that first year after I came back. It's running a bit wild now, but it's got some of the prettiest flowers—lilies and lavender, and a bush of yellow roses that the bees just love. And I've got me a hedge of sunflowers as tall as the house with bright, raggedy petals that wave in the wind, and seeds I save for the winter birds.

There's my white leghorns, too, that lay eggs like no hens I ever saw. They're so purely white they hurt my eyes sometimes when I see them in the sun.

I've even learned a bit about the stars. Not much because it's the sunsets I love, all those colors swirling around in the sky. Red, orange, yellow, like my lilies open to bursting. Some evenings Clay watches with me, and then I sit with him and wait for the stars. It's pleasant resting on the porch, knowing those stars will be there no matter what.

And the happiness? Well, maybe we're each given a little piece and that's all. Or maybe this here, me and this old man who took me back and never said a word against me, who never forced me or laid a hand on me till one day when I was ready, who kept me decent and bought me what he could to give me pleasure, maybe this here is enough.

Holy Water

I been working for the widow Crocker since she took
me in when I was sixteen. It was about then that I hit
the road away from home. My daddy was a mean man
and took his meanness out on anybody who happened
to be around when it hit him, including Ma. Well, she
was married to him. I wasn't.

He come at me that morning for some dumb reason,
but, instead of taking it, I turned and fought and left him
on his face in the dust. Then I packed my war bag,
kissed Ma, and headed south.

I was tired of those Colorado winters anyhow. Snow
and more snow, and hauling feed every morning and
night, and the cold so deep it like to steal the breath
right out of you. I figured the skiers were welcome to it,
all those rich folks from the East and California who
didn't have to earn a living and could sit around in front
of a fire all day.

So I come on south, hitching rides or walking, and
wishing I'd had the sense to steal my horse. I hit Arizona and looked around and didn't see one patch of
snow, which suited me fine. For a while I worked for a
rancher who had as nice a spread as I've seen, and then
took the notion to go on and see a little more. Hitched
a ride on a cattle hauler headed for a ranch near the
border, and, when I got there, I met the widow who was
running her own spread as good as a man, but who was
short-handed.

"You, boy," she said to me. "You lookin' for work?"

"Yes'm."

"Then go catch yourself a horse and get on down here and help load these cows."

"Yes'm," I said again, and sealed my fate.

That was twenty years ago, and we're still here, both of us, though the widow's got some age on her, had to go to the hospital for an operation, and that's when the trouble started.

There's not a thing about this place I don't know by now, and I don't cheat that old woman. She's been good to me, treats me like her own, but leaves me to do my own thinkin'.

This ain't a big spread, not like some—about twelve-thousand acres of good grassland and mountain pasture, and, between us, we've kept from over-grazing, cut down the herd during dry years, and we've had a spell of those lately. Had two winters without a drop of rain, so some of the tanks went dry, and we rationed our own water that comes from the well in the yard, just in case.

That's what I'm fixin' to tell about. Water. And the plain cussedness of folks who shouldn't be allowed to walk the same country, who should've been put out of their misery the day they was born, and save the rest of us a lot of trouble.

That's my opinion, and I've got a right to it, seein' as how they are, those Grumbles, and ain't that a name to make you think twice?

Anyhow, they come in here around five years ago, all fired up over that environmental stuff that we out here have known about for years, and straight off they started in on how us ranchers were killin' the earth, starving the wild animals, pumpin' the water out of the ground just to feed a passel of no-good cattle. They wasn't well liked, believe me, and, when they bought themselves a piece of land that joined the widow's, and proceeded to build what they called an "environmentally friendly house," I thought the widow would bust in two.

"Spyin' on us," she said, peering acrost the yard and the corrals to where the house roof poked up. "Just like a pair of buzzards, those two."

"We ain't doin' nothin'."

She sniffed. "If we aren't, they'll make something up. Make trouble. All these years I've done what I wanted on my own place, and now I've got bunny huggers crowding me."

Well, they moved in, and, first thing, they started leaving our gates open. Now, a cow or a horse knows by instinct about open gates, and they'll find it and go through, and pretty soon half the herd goes after, and you got a roundup you didn't need on your hands, plus neighbors pissed because your cows are on their grass.

The widow finally went over there and had her say, and they whined and squirmed and denied what they'd done.

"But it was them," she said to me, her eyes sharp as nails. "Both of 'em guilty as sin. They have some idea that the deer can't get to water over a fence."

We both had a good laugh at that one because a deer can jump over a church steeple if it's got a mind to.

"Are they dumb?" I asked.

"Just ignorant. Got their minds warped like some folks do about religion. And now they got some notion to make a habitat for birds."

"The birds already have one, seems to me." There must be a billion of the critters from hawks to herons and all the little ones in between, and I never give them a thought except once in a while to notice how pretty some of them are, or to watch those big herons standing still as sticks just waiting to catch a frog for supper. And now I'm remembering, there's no sweeter music anywhere than the song the white wing doves sing come spring.

"Why is it some humans got to meddle in what's already fine?"

"To keep the rest of us on our toes, I guess." The widow was lookin' far off, over the mountain, like she could see something I couldn't. "Sometimes I think the devil just likes to stir the pot a little bit. Makes us remember why we're here. Or maybe it's God who likes to see a good fight now and again." She looked at me then. "My granddad came out here and fought Indians for this place, and my parents made it through drought and the Depression. I reckon I'll survive the Grumbles, and you with me."

Looked at that way, I reckoned she was right.

Two days later, Mrs. Grumble drove up in her little toy truck. "There's a cow in my yard," she announced.

"Whose?" I asked.

She looked at me like I was one of those cow plops her kind get so hysterical over. "I didn't ask it," she said.

Lord, she was homely! I don't think I've ever seen a face like hers, not even on a salamander. That—and her attitude—got to me. "Well, now," I said, just as snotty as her, "well, now, why don't you just go back and do that?"

"Don't get smart with me!" She spit when she talked, and that didn't make me like her any better.

"If it's ours, I'll come get it," I said. "If it ain't, it's not my problem."

"It's . . . it's *pooping* in my yard!" My, she was mad, her face red as a beet. "It's *dirty!*"

I did my best not to laugh. "We all got to do it somewhere."

She stamped her foot. She had on some weird-looking shoes, like what you'd see on one of those astronauts. I noticed that, but didn't give it much thought then. Later, I was glad I had.

"You come get that creature right now! Or . . . or I'll have Chester poison it!"

"And you'll pay a fifteen-hundred-dollar fine. We got laws out here for folks like you. And as for that habitat of yours. . . ."

"Cooley!" The widow had come out and got in between us. A good thing, too. I never hit a woman in my life, but was gettin' close. "Cooley," she said, "go get the cow. We'll find out whose it is." Then she turned on the Grumble woman. "Now get off my place, and don't come back 'less you're invited. You've got a telephone. Use *it*, if you have a problem. And keep your little lily whites off my gates, or you'll find real trouble."

The widow is tough. And when she's riled, she looks—and is—dangerous.

"Don't you threaten me!" The Grumble woman stuck her nose so high up I thought she'd topple over backwards.

"That's not a threat. It's a promise," the widow said.

Well, it wasn't our cow, and I ended up pushing her over to the Triple O where she belonged, cussing all the way. *Dirty*, I kept saying to myself. *Dirty! Hell! It's just ground-up grass!*

We had a spell of peace after that, and the widow decided she'd better go get her knee replaced before it got so bad she couldn't sit a horse.

"You go," I told her. "I'll mind things."

"You're a good man, Cooley," she said. "Drive me in, and come back for me when it's done, will you?"

Well, I did, and come home and took care of a fence that needed fixing, and pushed fifty head up onto the summer range, and, all in all, I wasn't much around the home place except to sleep.

They kept the widow in the hospital longer than expected, some kind of complication, and then she spent another two weeks in therapy, so it was just short of a month when I drove in to pick her up.

"Good to see you!" She gave me a hug, and I was surprised at how little she was, no heavier than a mesquite twig.

"Let's go get us a decent meal," she said then. "The food I've been eating's like chicken scratch. I want grease and lots of it."

We went to a steak house, and that little woman chowed down like a hog. Made me hope I never had to go to a hospital. After that we ran a few errands, picked up groceries, and went on home. I thought she was going to cry when I pulled up at the gate.

"I'm not cut out for any place but here, Cooley," she said. "When my time comes, you see they don't take me."

"Count on it," I promised. "But your time ain't yet."

She sniffed. "Well, I know that. But I like to plan ahead."

I got the groceries in the house, handed her the stack of mail that'd come, and then went out to throw some hay to the horses. It wasn't but a little while that I heard her calling me. She was waving a piece of paper, all excited.

"You been pumping a lot of water while I was gone?" she wanted to know.

"No more'n usual," I said. "Probably less."

"You leave something running?"

I didn't know what she was getting at and said so.

"Well, just take a look at this." She shoved the paper at me, and I saw it was the electric bill. Now, I didn't know what her bill usually ran, but I did know that it don't take no nine hundred dollars to keep the house and barn going.

"Maybe the meter's busted," I said.

She sat there, looking worn out and fanning herself with the envelope. "Go and see. If the damned electric company's going to raise my rates like this, it'll break me."

We ran a tight operation. Nobody knew it better than me. "Seems like they'd have said, don't it?" I asked.

Well, I went out to the box and looked at the meter, and the little dials was zipping along like they was racing cars. There was no way we was pulling that much current. I stood there, puzzling over this a minute, then figured I was right, and the thing was busted and the bill a big mistake.

That's when I looked at the ground. Now the yard is hard-packed from trucks drivin' over, and us and horses walking around. Only some of that dirt looked like it had been dug up and put back nice and neat. And the next thing I saw was human tracks—not boots but funny-lookin', flat-footed and round-toed.

I bent down and scratched, and, sure enough, there was an electric cord, a heavy duty one, half buried. One end was plugged into the widow's outlet. It didn't take an Einstein to follow that cord across the yard to the fence. Once across, it lay there in plain sight until it disappeared in some kind of hedge in the Grumbles' yard.

I must've stood there for five minutes with my mouth hanging open, trying to figure how they come up with such a scheme, and just plain stunned that hypocrites like them were walking around on God's good earth.

"Well?" the widow said when I went back in.

"Get your jacket back on," I told her. "We're goin' to pay a little business call."

"Tell me."

I did.

"Well, god damn!" Now that woman hardly ever cusses, and, when she does, she's purely upset. Then she said: "I'm takin' my Derringer, and I'd advise you to take that Thirty-Eight you're so proud of."

"I might be tempted to use it, and then I'll be in jail and where'll you be?" I said, knowing I was getting mad. "Either that or they'll die at the sight of it, and you'll never get your money."

She snorted. "Bunch of pale-faced babies is what they are. All right, you can leave yours, but I'm going to have my say if I do have to pull my gun. You can trust me not to use it 'less I have to. Now get the truck."

When we pulled up in the Grumbles' yard, it didn't look like they were home, but that prissy little truck was there, so I pounded on the front door.

"You'll scare 'em off with that noise," she said. "Let's just go sniff around in back. I'd sure like to see where my money's been going."

Together we went around the side of the house, and then both of us stopped dead. Those Grumbles, for all their talk about saving water and loving the deer, had gone and made themselves a jungle in their own back-yard. I mean, there was a garden with enough vegetables to feed half the county, and flowers in raised beds, and fruit trees with about a hundred bird feeders hanging off the branches, and what looked like bird baths around underneath.

In the middle of it all, the Grumbles were blasting water on a patch of the greenest grass this side of a golf course.

"No wonder cows like to come here," the widow whispered. "Look at that damn' grass. It's cow paradise."

At that point the Grumbles turned and saw us, and the look on their faces would have been laughable if we hadn't been riled. They were like two kids caught stealing cookies.

"What a surprise! You're back home." Mrs. Grumble plastered on a grin so wide I could count the spaces between her teeth.

"I'll bet it's a surprise," the widow said. "I had a little surprise myself."

"You did?" Chester had come up and was standing beside his wife, probably thinking she'd protect him.

"This!" The widow reached in her pocket. "You been stealin' my electricity to pump your water, and you know it, so don't stand there tryin' to look innocent. You're both as crooked as sidewinders."

I started edging around on my way to the well, but Chester turned and grabbed my arm. "Don't walk on my grass, cowboy," he said.

Now, I don't take to anybody putting a hand on me, and I particularly don't like bein' called 'cowboy' in the tone of voice he was using.

"If you don't let go," I said, "I'm going to knock you

right into the mud on your fat ass."

"There are laws against violence. Even out here." Spoken like the true hypocrite he was.

I snickered. "You bet there's laws. There's laws about stealin' in particular, and you been stealin' this woman blind, and her not here to stop it. You come out here with your high-flyin' notions and act like you think you're some kind of god and above the law, but you ain't. You're a pair of skunks is all."

As I live and breathe, you won't guess what he said next. He said: "You're trespassing. Both of you. I demand that you leave."

Behind me, the widow laughed, as mean a sound as I ever heard. "I'll leave when I'm damned good and ready. And I won't be ready till you pay for what you stole plus damages. If that doesn't suit you, I'm sure the sheriff can change your mind. Of course"—she laughed again and sounded almost happy—"of course, I could just shoot the both of you and leave you for coyotes."

From the sounds that come out of those folks' mouths, I knew she'd pulled that Derringer.

"Shoot us!" they shouted together. "You can't!"

"Oh, I can. There's no law against shooting varmints. Least not that I know of. Now you go in and write me a check. I'll just keep the missus here till you come back."

"Do it, Chester! For God's sake!" All that woman's snotty behavior had been stripped away. For a minute I thought she'd start foaming at the mouth.

"Yes, do it, Chester," the widow mimicked. "And

don't think to come sneaking back to my place in the dark to remove the evidence. It'll wait for the sheriff. Besides, I'll be sitting up with a shotgun. Does a lot more damage than this pea-shooter."

Chester said: "This is unconscionable."

"It is for sure," I said, and gave him a push toward the house. "Now, git!"

"Go with him, Cooley, and make sure he doesn't get in any more trouble," the widow said without moving.

Inside, Chester sat down at a big roll-top desk in what I figured was an office. He had a fancy computer in there, and file cabinets, and a stack of what looked like bills, and on the walls were posters proclaiming long and loud about certain endangered species. A pity there wasn't a picture of the two of them alongside.

"This will break me," he said.

"You should have figured that out before you come up with your crazy notion. And what about that old lady out there? Didn't you think you might be on the way to ruining her?"

"She's loaded," he shot back. "That ranch of hers is worth millions, and you know it."

Truth to tell, I'd never put a price on the place, and I doubted she had, either. It was there, and we managed it the best we could like we'd take care of a child, like we cared for the animals that lived on it.

I said: "Your problem is you got nothin' to do. Nothin' to love, come to think of it." What I didn't add, though I was of a mind to, was that he wouldn't know what love was if it jumped up and bit him. All he knew was words somebody else had put into his head, while the widow's heart and soul was part of the place, and so was mine. It wasn't anything we'd ever talked about or spent our days discussing, it was just a fact in us, like our bones.

Watching Chester scribble out his check, I almost felt sorry for him—and for his wife. They was just poor, twisted humans, deaf and blind to what was around them.

He handed me the check, and I read it over careful, not trusting him the least bit. It looked proper, so I put it in my pocket. "If this bounces, we'll be back," I said. "You can count on it."

He screwed the cap on his pen—one of those fancy ink pens that cost a mint—and I wondered who he'd cheated to be able to afford it. "I don't write bad checks."

I'd have bet his life was paved with the suckers, but I kept my mouth shut having got what we wanted and knowing there wasn't no way I could make him into a decent sort. Sometimes you got to give up on what was a bad job to begin with.

"Try and behave yourselves," the widow told them when we were leaving. "It's not as hard as you think, getting along with your neighbors."

From their sour expressions, it was plain that they'd just had to swallow a bitter pill, and I laughed.

"Poor, misbegotten critters," she mumbled under her breath. "Bad as a two-headed calf."

We went off down the dirt road. It was about sunset,

and the mountains took on the last of the sun's fire like they do, turning red, as if they were burning from deep inside.

"Stop a minute." She put her hand on my arm.

We both sat there, then, lookin', fillin' our eyes with the pure beauty of the place, the colors of mountains and sky.

"We're lucky, Cooley," she said.

"Yes, ma'am, we sure are."

"For how long, I wonder."

"Long as we got eyes and the sense to use 'em."

She rolled down the window, and the smell of dry grass come in on the evening wind, and something else, like the way rain tells you it's coming from far away. It was dead quiet, just the sound of us breathin', the way it always is out here, so you feel like you been blessed.

She sniffed, reached in her pocket for a handkerchief, and I thought she was cryin'—not out of sorrow but because of the purely sweet rightness of the place.

After a minute, she folded her hands in her lap and sighed. "Folks like that can disturb your peace something awful," she said. "Now I'm tired thinkin' about them. Let's try and forget and go on home."

For Two Dollars

You see, it happened this way. . . .

Joseph Peña and I were out with the goats and sheep on the north side of the mesa where the grass was still green. We were young. And curious. And like all children we were bored staying in one place while the sheep grazed, the sun passed overhead, and the cottonwoods by the river did their dance in a breeze we could not feel.

Joseph lay on his back, staring at the steep cliff above us, and I felt the tension in him like a bowstring pulled back.

"What do you see?" I asked.

He squinted, his dark lashes covering most of his eyes. "A cave," he said. "There's a cave up there."

I looked, made out a small opening in the rock I'd never noticed, and that was strange. I have always seen the small things, always understood the voices of the earth.

"Let's climb up," I said.

"You might fall."

"I never fall."

Joseph, I understood, was just being a boy, acting tough, showing off his superior strength. He got up, stretched. "I'll go first."

It was a dangerous climb. The soft rock crumbled under our feet and finding hand holds was scary, but at last we stood on a narrow ledge with the small opening behind us.

I looked out then—across the yellow valley that shimmered between black, volcanic hills—and the beauty of the land was a sweet taste in my mouth, like honey from mesquite flowers. All around me that day there was magic.

Joseph was peering into the cave. "It's a little house," he whispered.

I knelt beside him and saw what he meant. In the roof of the round room was a small hole, a natural chimney, and light came in like the light of a lamp shining down on a fire pit so old that even the ash had turned to dust.

"Whose?" I whispered back.

"I think maybe the Old Ones."

I shivered. The Old Ones had lived in these valleys before our people came. What had happened to them, no one knew. But in that cave, on that hot, late summer afternoon, I knew they were still with us, that their spirits surrounded us like the dance of dust in the ray of light from above.

And I was even more sure of their presence when I saw the broken pot and gathered the pieces with their strange designs, black brush strokes on white clay. It seemed to me that the shards were talking, humming like a swarm of bees, making of the dark an enchantment that has stayed with me all of my life.

I filled my pockets to show Grandmother, who still made her pots in the old way, and who always took me with her to dig the clay from a place only she and

I knew. Then, when the buckets were filled, I would carry them home, walking slowly because they were heavy, and behind me, slower still, came Grandmother leaning on her stick, her face a map of earth with its seams and cracks, and her voice rusty with age.

"I learned this place from my mother. Now it's yours, but tell no one," she would caution.

I never have. I have only dug the clay for myself, taking the long way around and listening to the songs of earth—a spring of clear water, a thread connecting all things.

Joseph, that long ago afternoon, said: "Maybe you shouldn't touch anything. Maybe the old gods will be angry."

But I was determined. "These are mine," I said, fingering the cool, shattered pieces. "They've been waiting for me."

We walked home slowly, breathing in the dust kicked up by the sheep, both of us silent, thinking of those who had gone before.

Grandmother was under the elm tree that grew to one side of our house. She was washing and cleaning the clay we had brought back the day before, picking out sticks, stones, leaves, anything that would come between her fingers and the shaping of her pots.

I went and stood beside her, waiting for her to recognize me. After a minute, she smiled and patted the ground beside her. "Sit," she said. "Tell me what has happened."

In my hands the shards shone as if they had just been polished, and one by one she took them, studied them, put them in her lap.

"Where did you find these?"

I explained, and she nodded.

Then she asked: "Why did you bring them to me?"

It was a difficult question. There are times when, between the word in my mind and my mouth, there is a space in which nothing exists. And that day, as a child, I could not speak about what was in my head. I could not duplicate the reality so that Grandmother would understand.

"I . . . because. . . ." Speech was useless. With my hands I made the shape of a bowl in the air. "I want to do what you do, Grandmother," I said, and then was quiet, hunched into myself.

"Your mother needs your help. She'll be angry if you sit all day with me."

My mother was always angry, although she tried not to let it show. We were poor, and she worried about having enough to eat, about our debt at the trading post, about growing old and useless and still hungry.

Twice a year, though, my father took the wagon filled with the pottery Grandmother had made and drove to the train station where the white tourists came and bargained for her pots. Sometimes she got as much as fifty cents for a bowl or a jar, and once or twice a dollar. For a few weeks after, my mother was happy. Money paid for the food we couldn't grow, the things we got from the trading post where, most of the time, my mother's

165

jewelry was pawned until we could pay what we owed.

I picked a shard from the pile in Grandmother's lap. On it was painted a horned toad with a triangular head and wicked eyes that seemed to be making fun of me. It was easier to answer him than to describe what I felt inside.

"Someday," I said, "someday I will make pots that sell for two dollars."

Light gathered in Grandmother's eyes and touched the brown earth that was her face. She seemed like a *santo*, her head circled in gold.

"May it be so." She reached for my hand. "Now help me up. Tomorrow you can begin."

I remember how, on that first day, the clay began to speak. *I am this . . . bring me to myself. . . .*

First, as Grandmother showed me, I made the coils—long, damp snakes that wrapped around and around and that had to be kept wet so that the actual piece could be shaped.

"Thin as a cat's ear," Grandmother said. "Thin as the shell of a new-hatched bird."

Always, from that day, I listened to her and to the clay, learning when to stop, when to move on, making the growing life between my hands symmetrical—a word I didn't know then.

"Balance," Grandmother called it. "One side the same as the other, like what you see when you look at your face in the river."

I closed my eyes so nothing could come between us,

turned the birth shape between my hands, and let the voices come to me.

It was a kind of freedom but with always a price. Spin a form and you become that form. It inhabits you, and the debt you pay is to keep on, always attempting perfection but never achieving it, no matter if you live, as I have, almost a hundred years.

In the beginning, Grandmother was beside me—a presence like the Old Ones, a blessing like the summer rain—her hands guiding mine so that her spirit came into me, and her seeing that held everything she saw or knew in her aged body.

Of course, my mother was angry. She thought my apprenticeship was a waste of time, that I was bothering Grandmother and avoiding what she saw as real work—weeding, watering, tending the sheep, learning to cook our simple meals.

"Do you think white people need so many bowls and *ollas?*" she asked. "They have water that comes into their houses all by itself, and fancy plates, and their food comes out of cans. All you're doing is wasting time. No man wants a lazy woman for a wife."

I ignored her, even though what she said was partly true. I did what I did because I couldn't stop, each step in the doing bringing me closer to the heart of a great mystery. And besides, I had Joseph who, because he had been with me when we found the cave of the Old Ones, often came to watch Grandmother and me as we shaped and polished our work. It was Joseph who brought the wood for our fires, who gathered the manure used to smother the flames so that, somehow, those pots being fired turned black. I don't know why to this day, even though it's been explained to me. Grandmother never knew, either. That's just what happened. Some pots remained the color of the clay. Others, smothered by manure, turned black as the black, volcanic rock of the hills.

Just as at times there is an emptiness between thought and words, the same happens between desire and ability. When I started to paint my pots, I was a child with a vision I was too young to bring to life. How I struggled to control my hands, make them do what I wanted, drawing on ruined pots, on smooth rocks—struggled and cried from frustration.

It was Joseph who, one day, took up the yucca brush and drew a long-stemmed flower up the curving side of a jar—a graceful stem topped by yellow petals that came to life as if it grew there.

Grandmother nodded at him. "Where did you learn that?"

He shrugged and looked puzzled. "I don't know. It just came out of my hand."

His was a gift, always. What I did was through determination. My mother laughed her bitter laugh. "What kind of man wants to spend his life painting flowers? Next he'll be wearing a skirt! Tell him to go help his father and make something of himself."

But neither of us could help what we were, any more than a young bird can stop from flying. Joseph closed his ears to the taunts as if they were no more than pebbles tossed into the river, but I was hurt by them, by Mother's inability to understand the difference between herself and me. It was always so.

One morning Grandmother went to sleep under the elm tree, and her spirit flew up into the branches where the sparrows were building nests and the smoke from the fire was caught in the new leaves. And I wept because in her place was a space nothing could fill.

Joseph tried to comfort me, but I wouldn't listen. Finally he said: "You're just sorry for yourself. Not for her."

The way he spoke made me angry. "She wasn't your grandmother! How can you know what I feel?"

"Because I was there, too."

Oh, he was so sure of himself, standing outside the church where Grandmother lay in a wooden box, her hands still, her eyes closed to me forever.

"You're as bad as Father Roy," I said. "Him like a piece of wood saying prayers, giving blessings that don't mean anything. The same words all the time, over and over without thinking. What good do they do?"

He agreed with me. I could see it in his face, but all he did was reach into the sack he was holding. "I want to do something for her," he said. In his hands were two tiny jars we'd made as children. I remember how impatient we were as we waited for the fire to burn down, and how Grandmother scolded us in that gentle way she had.

"Sit still! Nothing happens before the right time. You

can't hurry the sun along, can you?"

"No," we said together.

"Well, then." She leaned against the tree and closed her eyes, and after a while she began to talk. It sounded like a prayer. "Take the time to look around you. To see things before they're gone and it's too late. Life is long, but it's short, too. One day you're a child, and the next you're old, and what went before is like a dream. When I look at you two, I see myself. I see another way opening, and it makes me happy."

While I had been seeing the past, Joseph had been watching my face. "Now do you see?" he asked.

I reached out and took one of the little seed jars. It fit in the palm of my hand. "You want to give them to her so maybe someday somebody will find them just like we did," I said, startled at the way I suddenly saw the flowing of life just as Grandmother had described it.

He took my free hand in his. "Come on. We'll have to hurry before Father Roy gets here."

Like two bad children we opened the carved church doors. Inside, it was cool and dark. Light came in from high overhead, a thin light that seemed to have passed through water, and a few candles burned, their flames dancing in the wind that came in with us.

We moved softly down the stone aisle, past the *santos* in their niches, past the handmade benches, the paintings of corn and sheep, lightning and rain on the walls that someone, a hundred years before, had made. The paint was flaking off now, and some of the pictures were only faint outlines, their colors faded, and I thought again of the shards that had lain in the cave for a thousand seasons.

What we do in life stays behind, just as what we say spins off into the sky but is never lost. A thread, invisible as the silk of a spider, connects us all, living and dead.

The lid on the coffin was shut with a few bent nails, but Joseph pried them loose. When I saw Grandmother's face, I stepped back, my legs trembling. She looked young and as if she were smiling. "She's not dead," I whispered, and it sounded very loud in the little church.

"Hurry up!" Joseph hissed. "I can't hold this open much longer. Anyhow," he added, "she's alive where she is."

Quickly I put the gifts in the folds of her best skirt and stepped back, my heart beating so loud my ears hurt. Just before Joseph fastened the lid, I heard Grandmother's voice from long ago.

Why did you bring these to me?

This time, my words came easily. "Because I love you."

Joseph bent the nails into place, looking solemn, and the slump of his shoulders made me sad.

I said: "Thank you. That was nice. A good thing to do."

"I loved her, too. She never scolded. She never laughed at me like the rest.

"I never laughed at you."

He reached out and took my hand. "Why would you? We're the same."

My mother caught us coming out of the church, her mouth a thin, dry line that broke her face into two pieces. "What were you doing in there?"

"Praying," I answered.

She gave us a hard look. "Pray when Father gets here. I need help. We have to feed him after the Mass, and who knows where the money's coming from? But maybe now you'll stop your foolishness, both of you."

Whatever had happened in the church, it had changed me forever. I shook my head, knowing Grandmother was still with me.

"No," I said, and my voice rang the way a good piece of pottery rings when struck. "Next week we're going to Santa Fé. If I make any money, you can have it to pay for whatever you want."

"A few dollars. Spent in a minute. How long did it take you to make those things? Six months? Five years?"

I was, I suddenly realized, taller than she was. I looked straight into her eyes and knew victory when she turned away. "It took me all my life," I said, then I, too, turned away.

So many white people! So many loud voices mixed with the sounds of horses and wagons and the new automobiles that fouled the air and made me long to be home again in the silence.

My father left me and Joseph to set up our display,

which we did, not talking to each other or to any of the rest who had come to sell jewelry that glistened like the sky, and rugs of many colors already spread out in the best places. We had come late, so we had only a little space at the very end of the *portal*.

I felt small, a person of no identity, an ant crawling across the sand of this city that, had I known it, was still a village, but which seemed to me to reach to the horizon. Shy, miserable, I sat looking at the ground, at my feet in their old moccasins, my hands, motionless in my lap.

What would happen to my painted children if they were not sold? What would happen to Joseph and me? We were in love, though we hadn't spoken of it, being young and just as hesitant about ourselves as we were about selling what we had made. The link between us was there, however, forged long before. We knew each other's moods and silences, strengths and weaknesses, as if we shared the same skin.

Oh, that day! Behind my eyes I can still see the men and women in their strange, white people clothes, and how the shadows of the trees in the little park in the center of the plaza, made crooked lines and patches of darkness on the sun-bright ground.

For a long time, I don't know how long, no one stopped to look at what we had, and I was discouraged, thinking maybe Mother was right, and the voices, even Grandmother's, had all this time been false.

Joseph was watching me as he always did. "Stop frowning, Angelita. The look on your face would frighten a bear." He laughed to make me feel better.

"They don't even stop." I was whining and hated it.

"They don't know how to see."

"I want to go home."

"Wait," he said. "We can't make anything happen."

Grandmother's words thrown back at me. I hated him. I hated how we sat there, like two beggars, our hands held out for white people's pennies. I said: "I'll smash everything."

He moved close to me. I saw his face, its roundness, like a bowl I could hold in my hands. "Stop it!" His voice was as sharp as a shard. "Remember who you are!"

That was hard. I was nothing but a dream.

"Oh, look! How sweet!" A woman stood in front of me. A woman with the face of a ferret, wearing a green skirt and buttoned boots that had never known the dust of a trail through the desert.

She picked up a bowl—my favorite—black on white with the old designs of mountains, lightning, patterns of clouds—that I had worked on for many months.

"How much?"

I hadn't been wrong. She did look like a ferret, all sharp nose and small eyes. My pride fought with desperation. I hesitated. The bowl was not meant for her. She'd treat it like a toy or something to be tossed out when she got tired of it.

I said: "Two dollars."

Her eyes turned into slits. "Fifty cents. You Indians think you can get away with anything."

Beside me, Joseph stiffened. He knew what I knew. That the bowl was my heart, and that I was angry. "Two dollars," he repeated.

The woman's laughter burned through me the way lightning burns into the core of a tree. "It's not for sale," I said.

Her thin lips turned in on themselves, and she tossed her head that had on it a silly, feathered hat. "I'll find something better," she said.

I nodded. Perhaps she would. But the bowl was still mine. When she was gone, when the sound of her little feet in those fancy boots had clicked away, I looked at Joseph.

"I'm a fool," I said. "I threw away money."

His smile softened the angles of his face. "No, Angelita. You must never sell the hours of yourself too cheap. Your grandmother wouldn't forgive you."

Relieved, dizzy, I closed my eyes. When I opened them again, a man wearing a dark suit and a wide-brimmed straw hat was standing there.

Slowly he knelt down, not caring that his knees were in the dust, and slowly he picked up the bowl. When he spoke, I heard the wonder in him. It pleased me. "You made this?"

My throat was dry as sand. I nodded.

"And this?" He lifted a jar with a slender neck.

Joseph answered for me. "She made them all. Some I paint myself."

One by one the man examined each piece, touching them as if they were sacred. *He understands*, I thought, amazed that there was such a person.

He sat back on his heels and looked at me, and from somewhere I found the courage to look back. "Are there more of these?"

Once again I nodded.

"It's what we do," Joseph said.

"This one . . ."—I found boldness and pointed to the black on white—"this one is two dollars."

A smile hovered at the corners of his mouth, and the pupils of his eyes became small black dots like I'd make with a drop of paint. When he spoke, it was slowly, as if he thought we wouldn't understand. "You're cheating yourselves. What you've done here . . ." He stopped and shook his head at what I assumed was our stupidity. "Three hundred dollars," he said at last. "For all of them."

Maybe he was crazy. Three hundred dollars would buy everything we needed for months, maybe a year. Joseph reached for my hand. He was thinking of marriage—and children who would not grow up shouted at or hungry. And a mother-in-law whose tongue would be silenced once and for all.

"These designs," the man was saying. "I've never seen them on contemporary pieces. Only in some of the digs."

"Digs?" The word was unfamiliar.

"Old sites. Where your people lived who knows how long ago."

"The Old Ones," I said with a smile.

"The Anasazi. The Hohokam. What they did. . . ."

Again he shook his head. "What they made out of nothing was magnificent. Is that what inspired you?"

Well, maybe. If inspiration means the reaching out to something that is nothing more than mist over the river on a cold morning, or the guidance of Grandmother's hands.

I said: "What they did . . . the Old Ones . . . was sacred. What we do is only an echo."

He looked as if he heard that echo, as if he was straining to hear the whole past and the future as it was shaped by the past. An unusual man, not like the rest of his people who came and saw what was on the surface like a photograph and went home thinking they understood all those who lived here and what the land was saying.

"Art can only *be* an echo." He expected me to answer, but I didn't know what he was talking about. He waited a minute, then said: "Don't you think so?"

If I understood, he was saying that my pottery was art. I thought art was the painting of pictures, if I had ever thought about it at all. It seemed we—he and I—were talking across a chasm, each of us bewildered by the other but needing to communicate. How to explain to him?

"I only do what I do because. . . ." I looked to Joseph for help.

"Because that's who she is," he said.

"But this speaks for all of us," the white man said, still holding my bowl as if it were a treasure—or a woman's body.

"This thing . . . this art," I said carefully, "it means that the voices choose you."

Those clever, half-yellow eyes of his lit up like the mesa in the morning sun. "It's a calling. For a few. You're one of the lucky ones."

How good it was to be known by a stranger! The happiness began in me in that moment, and it has never left. Not once. From that time, my mother's anger was like a wind that swept past and disappeared. From that time I began to see a larger and more compassionate world, a world full of people different from me and yet the same.

I heard the familiar rattle of my father's wagon before he turned the corner and stopped at the curb. He tied the team and came to stand beside me, all the time looking curiously at the white man.

Laughing, I said: "This is my father. Give the money to him."

Astonished, he stood there while my new friend counted out three hundred dollars. "What is this?" he asked.

"Give it to my mother," I said.

"She'll think we robbed somebody."

The white man chuckled. "Your daughter and her friend earned it. There will be more, I promise you."

Pride and disbelief fought in my father's eyes. Trust in white strangers was harder for him than for me, but finally he let himself smile. "Maybe so," he said.

The white man handed me a card with his name on it that meant nothing to me. Marks on paper, what are

178

they? A name is what is given. A calling is what is heard.

He said: "If I may, I'll come to see what else you have. Is it all right?"

I liked him—his eyes, the dust on his knees and worn boots, and how he held my bowl, with a kind of tenderness.

"You come," I told him. "We will be happy to see you."

I thought how my mother's face would be full of astonishment, how her hands would fumble over food for our visitor, and how her words would come out in no understandable order. She would look at me, her daughter, and see a woman she did not know, would never know, not if she lived a thousand seasons.

Sometimes birds hatch in a nest not their own. So it was with me who had been and would always be a stranger to her. Who knows why, for sure? But trouble is as necessary as happiness. It makes us strong; it speaks loudly of what we already know to be the truth.

And now, you see, how it happened to me. When the time was right, my life began.

Learning the Names of Things

There's a paloverde tree right outside my door, so close I have to duck under it coming and going. When I parked my trailer, I planned it that way because it's a pretty tree and interesting. Paloverde means "green stick," and the whole tree—trunk, branches, twigs—is green with hardly any leaves to speak of. When it blooms, it looks like yellow gauze, and the scent hangs on the air like the perfume department of a store at Christmas.

It's a miracle tree, but these days everything seems miraculous. I look, touch, smell the air, the earth, and its growing things, and then carry my sensations inside as if in a jewel box. No matter what, the contents are mine.

My name is Lily Crewes, but out here on the desert they just call me Lily. Nobody in our camp has a last name, and that's fine. It gives us all privacy, freedom, the most important thing of all. I'd guess that everybody here had their freedom attacked or taken away at some time. We're the walking wounded with bruised hearts, and instinctively as animals we've gone back to earth to be healed.

None of us talk much about our pasts or our wounds. In fact, we don't talk much at all. There's a silence here, part secrecy, part meditation, part a listening to the desert, a natural drug that sends us to sleep without dreams.

I'm a runaway wife. One of those you read about in

magazines that disappear without a trace so that no one knows if they're alive or dead. I suppose I might reappear someday just to make everything legal, but, then again, I might not. Anonymity is a glorious thing. Without an identity, without the protective colorations of house, husband, visible background, I can say what I want, be what I want with no comments. Take me as I am or leave me alone. It never happened to me before. Where I came from, everybody wanted to do a makeover of Lily, as if there was some basic lack in me that could be overcome with a lot of prompting and pushing and what amounted to a frontal lobotomy.

When I think about my life, and I often do, trying to make sense out of it by writing in my journal, my past seems like a kaleidoscope, a million pieces of jagged glass tumbling and abrading each other, with me, defenseless, in the middle. Did they draw blood, those knife-edged shards? Sure, but inside, where there was no visible scar, just shreds of Lily hanging in there because, no matter what, I knew life could be beautiful and probably was, some place else.

My mother raised me to be that nebulous creature, "a lady." I say nebulous because, the way she saw it, ladies weren't flesh and blood but fairy godmothers incapable of wrong-doing. If by some chance they erred, there were always the neighbor ladies and the governing body of the world at large to bring them back to perfection.

"What will people think?" was her standard, and, while early on I decided that people's opinion had nothing to do with anything, it colored enough of my behavior to get me into trouble in my marriage.

While I led myself to the sacrificial altar, the horror of old-maidhood, the snickers and gossiping of acquaintances, were pushing from behind. "Martyrs to somebody else's cause," is what my neighbor, Maggie, says.

Maggie lives down a little path and around the bend in a hodge-podge house she made herself out of old doors, damaged trailer siding, and pieces of tin roof. "Nobody's got a lock on construction," according to her.

We don't see each other often: some mornings for coffee, and once a month when I give her a ride to town to cash her Social Security check. I don't get checks. I've vanished. But Maggie has enough to make do. That's all she wants, she says. That and no one around giving orders.

My money—that I took from our joint account, Robert's and mine—is hidden under the floorboards of the trailer. If I'm careful, it will last a while yet, and I am careful. Me. Lily the consumer. That's what they used to call me—all those women who called themselves friends but who were as brain dead as I was. I used to buy in binges like a food addict—clothes, jewelry, dishes, napkins, towels, bits and pieces for the house, anything that looked good. I had taste, but that didn't count. It didn't cement the pieces of the kaleidoscope or stop Robert's voice from cutting deeper.

Robert is a professor of "Artificial Intelligence." He makes robots play chess and machines talk like people, but he can't talk like a person himself. During the seven years we were married, he became as much a robot as one of his creations, and acted like I was one, too—emotionless, programmed, incapable of feeling pain.

I'd be asleep, and I'd hear him coming after me, his voice like a buzz saw. "Lily, Lily, get up. Clean the stove . . . the tub . . . the cellar . . . wipe the mirrors, dust behind the pictures."

They've got a name for that kind of behavior now—obsessive compulsive—but then I never gave it a name or even thought about it. I was married. Stuck. Who would believe the "clean behind the pictures" bit? What would people say?

Besides, I was usually too exhausted to think at all. Brain dead. Numb. Abused, although I didn't call it that then.

And then I woke up. Just like that. I caught myself in mid-stride rushing out my own front door to do an errand and get back in time to finish the list of chores Robert always left for me. It was a day for rejoicing, but I wouldn't have noticed except that a cardinal flew past me, landed on a bush, and sang his scarlet heart out.

How many springs had come and gone and me on my knees, mopping? How many sunrises had I missed learning to make perfect eggs and oatmeal, and measuring tea with precision into Robert's Wedgewood pot? How many daffodils? Soon I'd be old—I could die tomorrow—and what had I done? Seen? Listened to? I was a stranger to my own heart.

I went back inside, smoked a pack of cigarettes, and

thought. I thought for days. Robert didn't notice.

I noticed him, though. I saw things I'd never seen before. He pouted at dinner when the food displeased him, which was often. He was paranoid. He believed the telephone company was after him because I mailed the payment a day late. He was a slob. He left his clothes, both dirty and clean, in piles on the floor for me to sort. He was possessive, selfish, and completely humorless. Even his laughter was fake. "Ha, ha," he'd go, and then look to see if the rest of the company was laughing.

It was his feet that did it, though. They were ugly and big, and, when he walked, the floors shook. I could hear him coming—*bang, bang, bang*—like King Kong, and it scared me. *He* scared me. Sometimes when he hugged me, he left bruises on my arms, and, when I cried out, he laughed and said: "Oh, you're too fragile." This was love? Not in my book.

So I sold my jewelry, emptied the checking account, took the Cadillac, and left. I drove off into the sunset and never stopped until I hit the desert. It felt like home. I looked at all those fragile cacti, at those naked rocks sticking up like my own bones, and I said: "This is it. This is where I live."

Only I couldn't live in a fancy hotel or in one of the big cities. Professors like Robert travel a lot to conferences where they eat well, stroke and steal each other's inventions, and gossip, while their wives shop, take tours, and indulge in their own back-biting gossip. Sooner or later, I'd be found.

So I scouted around out in the bush and found what reminded me of a hobo camp in the Depression, except there were women, too, nice women who smiled and offered me coffee cooked over a wood fire or a propane burner. They didn't ask me any questions, and I didn't question them, either.

I went out and traded the Caddy to a Mexican used-car dealer for this pickup and little trailer that looks like a mushroom, and set up housekeeping. Me and the Hippie. I found him at the side of the road, squatting in a pile of weeds, and I thought he was a Yorkshire terrier until he started to grow. He turned out mostly Irish wolfhound. A big difference, but he's good company and keeps strangers away.

What do I do with myself? I keep this journal. I hike. The Hippie and I have covered the washes, the valley, the sides of the mountains. I walk with a book of birds or flowers in hand so I can learn the names of things.

Once you learn what something is called, you've got power over it. The Indians believed that, and the slaves in the South. They all had secret names that nobody knew, and that meant there was a part of themselves that belonged to them and was free.

That's why nobody here has a last name, or, if they do, it's a made up one. I wonder if I'd had another name, would it have helped me? If I'd told Robert that my name was a secret, that I was someone other than Lily and that he was neurotic, would it have helped? I already know the answer. He'd have said everything was my fault.

I go to bed when I'm tired, and wake up when I feel like it. I watch the sun rise through the paloverde branches, and there's something about the beginning of day that leaves me breathless. First the night lifts off slowly, and the trees and mountains take on their daytime shapes. The sky in the east turns green, then red, catching fire, burning hotter and hotter—red, orange, yellow-white, and, just when you think you can't stand the beauty or the suspense, the whole sky cracks like an egg and the sun is born, spilling down the cañons in a river of light.

Nights are different. Mysterious. Cold. Enchanted. When I can't sleep, I watch how earth changes in moonlight. The tree casts a thousand tiny shadows. There is an owl hooting, and coyotes chuckling in the wash. When he hears them, the Hippie pricks his ears and howls like he wants to join them, except he hasn't been invited, and he's very polite. I'd like to tell him: "Go on! Run! Catch a rabbit! Find a nice lady coyote all yellow-eyed and sassy, and prance and grin and make funny puppies."

I don't say it, though. There are too many orphans in the world as it is. I'm glad Robert and I were childless. We'd have made a mess between us, and who needs more mixed-up kids? We can't handle the ones we've got.

I think a lot, too. I guess that's obvious. All of the facts I took for granted have come under the microscope. There are as many of them as there are rocks on the desert, and as many evils lurking underneath. I've had to think each accepted rule through from beginning to end, learning what's true for myself.

Take Loper, for example. Unless I miss my guess, he's an ex-con or a prison escapee living in a place that's part dug-out, part tent, part tin cans laid sideways and glued together with the unopened ends facing out. They catch the light and shine in your eyes, making Loper hard to see when he's sitting under the mesquite tree skinning rabbits and cleaning his .45. Nobody sneaks up on Loper. He was raised on an Indian reservation in Montana, and he learned all the tricks.

When I first came, he walked up the trail early one evening carrying an old iron pot. He was the ugliest man I'd ever seen, the kind my mother told me to run from if I was so unlucky as to meet him in a deserted alley.

Most of his front teeth were missing, easy to see because he carried his lips in a kind of snarl that was supposed to be a smile. I knew this because the Hippie does the same thing every once in a while; in fact, at that moment, he was doing a fine imitation.

"Nice night," Loper said, stopping two feet away and planting his legs like logs in the sand.

"Yes," I said, fascinated by seeing so many tattoos at close range. They streamed down his arms all the way to his knuckles—mermaids, cobras, sharks, poisonous orchids, God knows what.

"I made too much stew. It won't keep." He held out the pot, and I could smell the savory contents. "Since you just come, I thought I'd be neighborly."

He reminded me of a rattlesnake. Poke him and he'd coil. Otherwise, he was fine. "Thanks," I said, disregarding all my mother's edicts. "Want some coffee?"

"Naw. Too hot. I'd take a beer if you got one."

"Sorry," I said. "I'll stock up in town in a few days."

"Beer's the thing," he said. "Keeps down the dust." He turned and started down the trail, then stopped. "I'm just down here when you're done with the pot."

He looked like he felt foolish. Like he'd overstepped some invisible boundary. Surely a man like this one didn't worry about things like that.

"My name's Lily," I said.

His eyes brightened. "Loper," he said. "That's me." He rumpled the Hippie's fur. "Who's the mutt?"

"The Hippie. I found him in the weeds a couple months ago. Somebody must've dropped him."

He stared at me with those green glass eyes. *Lord*, I thought, *he's a killer*.

He said: "People suck."

"So what else is new?" I answered, and he laughed.

"Not too damn' much. But it's nice, you keeping the dog." With that benediction, he bobbed his head and disappeared around the bend.

The stew was delicious. I wanted the recipe. The next morning I scrubbed the pot till the crust came off, called the Hippie, and went off down the path.

As I went, I noticed bird tracks in the sand—quail, probably, and lots of coyote prints. I was studying the ground when Loper materialized from behind a creosote bush and stopped beside me.

"Lots of traffic last night," he said. "Lucky it wasn't the Feds. How'd you like the stew?"

"Well enough to want the recipe."

He lifted his lip. "Well, now," he said, "well, now, I dunno. You *sure* you liked it?"

"Sure, I'm sure," I said, wondering what the catch was. "What was in it? Rattlesnake?"

"Gophers," he said.

Fortunately I'd digested it all. I think I just turned white.

"I knew you'd puke if you knew what 'twas," he said. "But you liked it, didn't you?"

I nodded, afraid to open my mouth.

"It's an Injun recipe. Had it since I was a kid. But it won't do you no good 'less you can trap the gophers."

"Never mind," I said. "Here's your pot. I cleaned it up."

He took it and looked at it like it was going to bite him. "Damn," he said finally. "Took me years to get that flavor on it."

"You mean that mess I scrubbed off?"

"Yeah, but don't worry. I got another."

"I'm sorry," I said. "I didn't mean to ruin it."

"Forget it. Your ma raised you right."

I looked up into that fierce, ugly face. "Loper," I said, "my ma didn't raise me to know a single thing that counted."

"Hell, kid. She didn't know. She just thought she did like everybody's ma."

If that were true, then everybody had been or was in

my predicament. Taking baby steps at age thirty-five, or maybe never. If that were true, then we all raise our-selves or don't, and, if we don't, we find somebody who will. We marry them and call them "husband" or "wife." The thought was horrible. All evidence to the contrary, I'd married my mother.

"I've got to go," I said. "Come by for a beer."

"I sure will." He tossed the pot in the brush and dis-appeared the way he'd come. It was uncanny how he was able to do that. I wanted to learn how, too. Maybe I'd need to disappear someday. I picked up the pot. It was a good one. Some things I learn fast.

I was sitting under the paloverde trying to convince myself that, even though Robert had acted like a nag-ging mother, it didn't mean I'd been guilty of incest, when a woman came up the trail, all arms, legs, and a braid of hair hanging over one shoulder.

"Howdy," she said, looking around and appraising my trailer.

I'd never said "howdy" to a living soul. I thought only movie cowboys talked like that. I repeated the greeting and hoped I didn't sound like a dude. I was after pro-tective coloration.

"Loper said you'd moved in. I'm Maggie."

"Lily."

"Nice to meet you." She stooped and let the Hippie smell her hand. "Loper said you were a real lady."

There was that word again. Even ex-cons seemed fond of it. "Is that good or bad, do you think?"

"Depends," she said. "You have a spare cigarette?"

I tossed her my pack. "Keep them if you're out."

She ran her fingers over the top of her head like she was plucking out her brains. "I'm trying to quit," she confessed. "I really am. But, honest to God, it's hard. Maybe I shouldn't. What do you think?"

I'd been through that struggle. "Everybody's got to go some way. Dealer's choice."

"Now that's a fact. That's a real fact." She lit up, inhaled, exhaled, and watched the smoke rise through the tiny green twigs. Then she grinned. "You've convinced me, kid. I might die horny, but I'll be damned if I'll go wanting a smoke."

We sat a while in silence, looking at the sky. Then she tucked the pack inside her T-shirt. "I'll pay you back on pay day," she said. "See you around. I'm just past Loper's, if you need anything. Us women should stick together."

"Yeah," I answered, not wanting anything to do with women.

I was still stuck on the mother question. Maybe Robert had thought I was *his* mother, that old harridan who'd moved in on us and finally died in our third floor bedroom out of pure malice. It was hell getting her body down the narrow back stairs.

Did all this make me a creep? I wasn't sure. I'm still not sure. After all, morons can't know they're morons, so how can creeps tell?

Pondering all these matters got me through the summer and into the fall. Gradually I met the rest of the camp dwellers: Lorene and Carl who are married, dress alike in ragged roadrunner T-shirts and caps labeled THE OLD FART and THE OLD FART'S WIFE; the man we call Father Frank because he feeds the birds and they're always around him like Biblical doves. Personally I think he's a runaway priest, having seen him pacing back and forth like he's saying Angelus, and having noted in his dark eyes a reserve typical of all the priests I ever knew. As in "Don't touch me, I'm holy." I always believed I could talk to God all by myself without using anyone else as a medium. I still believe it. Out here on the desert I talk to God every day. Like the Indians, I believe He's in the wind, the sky, the mountains. It makes it easy to pray.

This brings me to the medicine man, Jim Turtle, who walks around shirtless and who's usually out in a cañon meditating over a tin can filled with burning herbs or smoking on a pipe decorated with beads and feathers. I stopped one day, mostly because I was tired of talking to myself, and because he'd aroused my curiosity.

"Howdy," I said, congratulating myself. I sounded good. Like a native.

He turned and focused on me like I was five miles away. He said: "How."

Indians don't really say that, or, if they do, they shouldn't. Coming from him, it sounded hokey. I sniffed the aroma of herbs and asked: "What're you smoking?"

"You want a drag, white woman?" he answered.

I could hear my mother's voice loud and clear. For

once, she was right. "I've got to go," I said. "Thanks anyhow."

"You look like you got problems. You want to go in the sweat lodge, you come tell me. Jim Turtle." He smiled, looking purely evil.

"You watch out for him," Loper said when I repeated the conversation. "He's bad medicine. Attracts women like a pile of shit brings flies."

"That doesn't sound nice," I said, recalling how, in childhood, the word "shit" was never spoken in my mother's presence.

"It ain't supposed to. I grew up with Injuns, and he's a bad one if he even is an Injun. I bet he's from Brooklyn."

"Now how would you know that?" I asked.

"I was in the Navy."

"What's that got to do with it?"

"Stationed in Brooklyn," he said.

Out of some deep-rooted desire for mischief, I said: "He wanted me to go in his sweat lodge."

Loper's eyes turned that hard, killer green. "I'll sweat lodge him. Don't you go."

"I never intended to. I just thought it was funny."

"Ha," he said without humor. "If he bothers you again, you tell me."

"He didn't bother me. I just asked what was he smoking."

Loper threw up his hands. "Don't you know better than to go around asking guys that? You're a damn' fool, and that's the truth."

193

Actually I didn't know better. When it comes to people like these, I'm as green as the trunk of the paloverde. "Common," my mother would have called them, dismissing in two syllables the possibility that they bore any resemblance to her own person or to mine.

I'm beginning to pity her. She missed out on the fun. These people are fun. Alive. Vital. Interesting, even though they stick to the brush like quail. Better that than inside a twelve-room house decorated by some gay according to his taste and not mine. Better out here than almost anything I can think of.

What makes a home? It isn't necessarily four walls and a roof. Jim Turtle sleeps in a wickiup; the priest in a blue canvas tent. I read recently about a bag lady who refused to leave her beat and go into a shelter. She said she liked her life the way it was.

As for me, I've put down roots like a desert plant, down through layers of sand and rock to where the water runs cold and clear, only the roots exist in my mind, not in the place. I could live anywhere, and I guess I'll have to.

Right after Thanksgiving, which came and went without anybody noticing because people on food stamps aren't much into holidays, and because out here we don't look at the calendar, Jim Turtle began digging into the crumbling banks of the wash just like his name-sake. He made a kind of dug-out that he roofed over and fronted with yucca stalks and weeds, and then he car-ried rocks inside—big ones, big enough to rupture most men. He didn't seem to notice their size, just flexed his muscles and kept humming to himself.

I found him, sitting beside his little room one day, when I was coming back from a walk. I wouldn't have seen him except that the Hippie's hackles went up and he growled. That dog hated Jim, for what reason I didn't know, except that Loper said dogs have an instinct about people, and the Hippie knew Jim was no good.

"What's that you built?" I asked out of simple politeness. My upbringing again. Always be nice to people.

He tipped his head back to see me better as I stood above him. "Sweat lodge," he said. "Some folks in town want to try it. You can try, too. Just come on down. Leave the mutt at home." He started to get up. The Hippie growled harder.

"That dog's nuts. You know that?"

"He's OK."

"Woman like you needs a real dog."

That put my back up. What did he know about dogs or about women like me? I smiled my most condescending smile learned at my mother's knee.

"Smart ass," he said, and sat down with his back to me.

"Dumb son-of-a-bitch," I yelled at his head.

Loper materialized out of a cactus a few yards farther on. "Now that's real nice. You sound like you grew up in a pool hall."

It was happening again—the remaking of Lily. I freaked out. "Who're you? My mother?"

195

"Somebody's got to keep you out of trouble."

"I can take care of myself."

"Yeah," he said. "What'll you do when you wake up some night and find him in your bunk?"

"He wouldn't dare."

Loper raised his lip. "Don't count on it, sweetheart."

I went fuming to Maggie's. "I thought people out here minded their own business. It seems like everybody's minding mine."

She drew a bead on me with her blue eyes. "Hell, kid, they've never seen anybody like you before."

Didn't I fit anywhere? Was I always going to be out of place? "What's so different about me?" I cried. "I'm just me."

"Like Loper said . . . you're a lady." She lit a cigarette and waved it at me, cutting off my protest. "Calm down and listen. You come in here and expected to have it all your own way, but nobody has it like that, not even here. You're young, you've got money or seem to, and you're pretty. What'd you expect with a bunch of horny guys, a serenade? They're snuffing your tracks like a bunch of hounds, Loper included, and they can't help it. The trouble with men is women. And vice versa."

I grasped at the one word that made sense. "I'm not pretty," I said. I believed that to be true. No one had ever commented one way or the other on my looks, probably to guard me from conceit. Even Robert in the sentimental days before our marriage had remained silent on the subject. His one flattering remark, if such it was, was that I had nice arms.

Maggie snorted. "Oh, Lord, look in the mirror!" She had a small glass tacked on the wall, and she pushed me at it.

I looked and saw my face. Eyes, nose, mouth, all in a line like everybody else's. I shrugged. "Nobody's making sense around here. Not even you."

She backed off, belligerent as a cat. "You don't think?"

"No. All I see is everybody with a finger in my pie, and I've had that up to here."

"Well, now," she said, drawing herself up, "well, now, you go ahead and do it on your own, then. Only don't come running to me every time you want answers."

So I went home, and a week passed without my seeing a soul. I caught glimpses of the others, but they kept to themselves. By the end of the second week, I was lonesome. I hadn't talked to anybody but the Hippie, and he never answered. So I was almost glad to see Jim Turtle coming through the mesquite toward me. The sunlight gleamed on that chest of his like he'd painted himself with bronze oil. He probably had. Close up, he looked like a collage with parts added here and there. Even his braid seemed like an afterthought.

He showed his white teeth. "How," he said.

The Hippie rumbled in his throat, and his eyes, focused on Jim's belly button, looked like an alligator's.

Hoping to keep him at a distance, I said: "Yes?"

He steam-rolled right over my fragile barrier. Lady-like behavior had no effect on him. "How'd you like your picture in the paper?"

All I could think of was Robert's reaction if he should see me, Lily, on the front page surrounded by half-naked oddballs. "No, thanks," I said. "I take terrible pictures."

He snickered and squatted down and drew lines in the sand with his finger. "They want to write about my sweat lodge in the paper. I thought it'd look good . . . you standing out front."

"There must be a lot of women you could ask," I said. "You don't need me."

He stopped drawing and looked at me. "But you got yellow hair." He sounded wistful, like a kid full of dreams.

I thought fast. He probably pulled that sad act on all the girls. I looked back into those bottomless dark eyes. "Why don't you put an ad in the paper?"

He was on his feet in one fluid motion. "You think you're so cool," he snarled. "Coming in here like Missus Socialite slumming. Looking at us like we're some kind of experiment." Then he reached out and grabbed a handful of my hair.

The Hippie went for his arm. I opened my mouth and yelled like a Comanche, and, when he loosened his hold, I grabbed Loper's old pot and clobbered him. I missed knocking him out—he was quick—but I connected with his ribs until the pot rang like a church bell.

He was backing down the trail as fast as he could with the Hippie hanging onto his leg and me swinging away

198

when Loper charged up and wrapped a tattooed arm around his neck. He dragged him around the bend, with the dog still clinging. It was hard to tell who was growling loudest.

I was ready to follow and finish what I'd started, when the shock hit me. Not the kind of shock you'd expect, either. I wanted to kick him, gouge out his eyes, yell over the body. I could feel the blood in my veins, the heat of the earth in the soles of my feet. Strength boiled up like a lava flow, and suddenly and completely I understood why men love war and struggle to conquer mountains. At the same point I wondered what was wrong with me and all the women I'd known who trembled at harsh words and hid under the bed and the smallest sign of violence. Where had all the Amazons gone?

I was sick and tired of misconceptions, of people seeing me as wallpaper. I was alive. Life was precious. So was I. I was laughing when Loper came back, blowing on his knuckles.

"You did good, kid," he said. Then he squinted at me. "You hysterical or something?"

"Nope."

The Hippie ran past us with what looked like a black snake trailing from his jaws. Loper gestured with his thumb. "He got the scalp. Didn't I tell you he was a fake Injun? His hair's red as Bridie Murphy's."

"Let's have a beer," I said, wanting to celebrate my new found self.

We sat a while in silence, drinking and absorbing the

sun like a couple of lizards. Then he said: "I reckon you found out some things your ma never told you."

"I guess I've been hiding out most of my life."

He drained his beer and popped open a second. "Better late than never, as they say."

Around us the desert shimmered with light and the swaying of branches. From one of them a thrasher whistled—"*Phew!*"—like a come-on. In the distance, another answered. Like the Pied Piper, they seemed to be calling me.

I said: "I wish I could stay."

"Hell, kid. You got things to do with your life. The rest of us . . . well . . . we've kinda run out of gas."

I stared at the mountains that ringed the horizon. Beyond them was more desert. Other mountains lifted their shoulders in the distance, and beyond them was California with its movie stars and earthquakes, and hippies who read poetry in coffee houses, smoked more dope than Jim Turtle, slept around. I had never slept around. I didn't know how to begin. It seemed I knew less now than when I had started.

The little encampment had become home, even if its people were has-beens. All I could say for myself was that I had never been much of anything at all. "Loper," I said, "it's big out there."

His eyes went hard, then soft again. "I'm bettin' on you," was all he said.

"I'll miss you." That was the truth. Leaving Loper was harder than leaving Robert had been.

Sentiment didn't sit easy on Loper. He looked like he

wanted to be some place else. He grunted.

"I'll tell you what," I said, grasping at straws, hating to cut my traces. "Live in my trailer. That way I'll know there's a place to come home to."

He grunted again, emptied the can. "Sure, kid, if that's what you want. But you won't be back. Just go on and keep your nose clean." He got up, ruffled my hair the same way he ruffled the Hippie's, and went off down the trail.

Now I'm loaded up and ready to go. The Hippie's riding shotgun. I'm touching the paloverde tree like I can take it with me—green, thorny, tough. I'm looking at the blue cloud shadows, the heat waves dancing in the air, and I'm feeling the way the pioneers must have felt heading West. The women, too. They didn't get here by pulling fainting spells, putting on airs, worrying about the neighbors. They had more important things to think about. Like survival. They did what they had to do, and, if they shed tears over being uprooted and leaving loved ones, they did it in silence, inside where no one could see. In their pockets they carried seeds to plant to remind them of home.

I pick a pod from the tree. It is boat-shaped like a dry pea, and, inside, the seeds shiver when shaken. I put it in my shirt pocket, get in the truck, and slam the door.

Call me Lily Appleseed, off to make a little history of my own.

The sign read SAN FELIPE. ONE MILE. Jack Roman slowed his truck and peered down the highway. In the late afternoon light the little town seemed a mirage, a painting on the rough canvas of the mountains, an abstraction of planes and angles jumbled on the valley floor.

He was tired. And hungry. His legs, those twisted things held together with pieces of metal and clever grafts of skin, bone, and tendon, ached from sitting too long. He wondered if there was a diner in San Felipe or if he'd have to push on another hundred miles before finding a meal and a place to stop for the night.

The road curved, then straightened, bisecting the town. On the west side, set back, was a tourist court that looked like it had been there since the 'Twenties. Overshadowing it was a water tower with bold lettering: SAN FELIPE ESTABLISHED 1900.

Old adobe houses lined the other side, some with small, tree-shaded front yards. He passed a garage and gas station, a post office, a tavern that was closed, a general store and café. Behind that he saw a church spire, sharp against white clouds and blue sky. A flock of pigeons came from nowhere, wheeling and circling around it, their wings catching the sun, and the hunger that filled him then was not of the body but an ache for a life lost and beyond recapture. There was before Vietnam, and there was after, and after was a kaleidoscope of loss, pain, visions that came and went and left Jack Roman spinning directionless as a top without a string.

"We don't go there."

Since his release from the hospital, he'd formed the habit of talking to himself like he was two persons split in half. Usually it worked, brought him back into reality, into the present, such as it was, a present without a center, without Mary Anne.

He whispered her name, then slammed on the brakes. If the café was still open, he'd eat, then decide where to go next, if anywhere. When you had no set destination, when you were running only to keep from standing still and being hit, one town was the same as another, and the country was vast.

Fifty miles to the south, Raul Figueroa drove into a narrow wash, cut the motor of the old Toyota, and sat listening. He heard only a cow, bawling in a mesquite thicket, the *buzz* of a fly, the flick of wind against his ear.

Up ahead, in an abandoned miner's shack, five Chinese illegals were waiting. Each had handed over one thousand dollars for him to smuggle them into the U.S. He smiled to himself. Not bad for a night's run. And it would be night before too long.

He got out of the truck and walked up the wash. It was possible to miss the shack, shaded by a stand of cottonwoods and tucked beneath an overhang, its boards weathered the color of rock and earth. A good place, as yet undiscovered by the law, he had used it often.

Whistling softly, he rapped three times on the sagging door, then pushed it open. The Chinese were huddled together, four men and a girl, filthy, exhausted, frightened if the look on their faces was anything to go by. It was hard to tell, but then they all came to him scared, like rabbits that knew the hounds were hunting them. Usually, though, he could talk to them. This bunch was different. They spoke no language he'd ever heard.

"Come on," he said, then gestured.

Silently they picked up their sacks and followed, clinging together like school children, stumbling and shielding their eyes as the sun struck them full-strength.

Back at the truck, he fished a jug of water from behind the seat and handed it to the one he figured was the leader. Again, it was hard to tell, they all looked young and lost. He shrugged. Not his business. Nor was it any concern of his what happened once he dropped them off. He gave them a day, two at the outside, before they either died in the desert or were picked up and sent home, a lot poorer, but that wasn't his problem, either. His part of the deal would be done within a couple hours.

"Get in," he ordered before realizing they wouldn't understand. "Shit!" He grabbed one of the boys and shoved him into the rear space, then pushed in two others and tossed them a blanket.

They crouched on the floor like sick dogs and watched him out of eyes that never blinked.

"Cover up!" Strangely they did. No telling what they understood except that they knew to hide.

The girl and the oldest boy scrambled into the front, the girl between them. He could feel her trembling and was annoyed. Did she think he'd rape her with the stink of sweat and *Dios* knew what else on her?

Women were all the same, thinking they were desirable even after they got old and fat. Did this one know what she looked like, this Chink with her hair cut so short he could see the bones of her skull, her face round as a melon and smeared with dirt? Besides, she was scrawny—built like a sparrow—and he liked his women full-breasted, scented with perfume.

Ignoring her, he switched on the ignition and shifted into reverse. The tires spun in the deep sand, spun again, digging deeper, then slowly found traction. Next week he'd get new tires. By the time they wore smooth, he'd be out of the coyote business and living like a *rico*.

Next year. It was a promise. *Next year*.

In spite of her fear and exhaustion, the girl recognized his revulsion and its reason, and anger as bitter as bile rose in her throat.

Mexican pig! What could he know of the life left behind, the soldiers that came in the night and took her father, her mother buried in an unmarked grave without prayer or proper ceremony? How could he understand the desperation, the long journey fueled by hope, with fear always snarling at her heels like a rabid dog?

What did he know of her reasons for being here in this wasteland, dependent on him for her freedom? She wanted to weep, to curse, to spit out the vile taste in her mouth but, instead, forced herself to sit motionless, staring straight ahead at the nearly invisible track through the desert.

They drove through a cañon with rock walls that rose straight on either side, and she thought she had never seen anything as forbidding, as hostile as those naked mountains, the boulder-strewn path that seemed devised to block their way.

When at last Raul turned onto the highway that cut through an immense and grassy valley, she sighed once, a tiny sound lost in the sound of the wind coming through open windows, and for a moment she closed her eyes.

Raul relaxed and let his mind wander, reached for a cigarette and lit it, inhaling with pleasure. It was dusk now, and the road was empty, the border patrol home filling their bellies. From here it was a straight shot.

When he got home, Clara would be waiting, worried as always that something had gone wrong. But nothing had ever gone wrong. He was too clever, like the animal for which he and the others like him were named—coyote—quick, smart, elusive as shadow.

Only a few hours now. A few miles more.

From her seat behind the counter, Liz Jerome watched the man get out of the truck and limp across the highway. She thought he looked like one of the sunken-eyed images that hung in the church—a saint who had been tortured, and, although she'd been about to close for the night, thought better of it.

People interested her. Their talk and observations of places beyond the valley she now never left were her newspaper, her encyclopedia, a way of understanding the world, and these days it took a lot of understanding.

"Jilly!" she called, and a tall Navajo woman in a white apron came out of the kitchen.

"What?"

"Don't shut down yet. We've got a customer."

Jilly turned and looked out, then said: "There's not enough food in the state to take this one's hunger away." Her father had been a *hatali*, a medicine man, and sometimes she saw things ordinary humans missed.

"You're probably right. Again." Liz leaned her elbows on the counter.

"I am." Jilly's minor key voice was mournful. "He's been crucified. And don't you go feeling sorry. You have enough troubles."

Liz chuckled. "I'm fine. I just have trouble when you start getting your religions all mixed-up together."

Jack ducked his head under the *portal*, came down the access ramp, and stepped inside. Then he stopped and stared at the huge room with its dark ceiling beams and white walls hung with rugs of various patterns and colors. One half was given over to rows of canned goods, cold storage and a freezer, bins of fresh vegetables, stacks of blankets, saddles on racks, bridles hanging from pegs. The other side held an assortment of wooden tables and chairs and terra cotta urns filled with green plants. Sunlight poured through the windows that faced west, and it seemed to him that he'd stepped out of one world and into another, happier one, a place that smelled of cinnamon and cloves, onions frying in butter, sweet bread dough.

"Hi, can I help you?" Liz was smiling. Her eyes, a pale aquamarine, caught the light and shone.

Hot, tired, dusty, needing a shave, and suddenly awkward, he took off his hat. "Is the restaurant open?"

"It is now. Have a seat. Anywhere."

He did as he was told, and was shocked when she wheeled herself out from behind the counter. She ignored the look on his face. God knew she was used to that by now. "Coffee's hot. Want some?"

"Please."

"Jilly!" she called over her shoulder. "Any soup left?"

"Soup, chicken sandwiches, one piece of lemon meringue pie," came the answer.

"Sound good?" She set the coffee on the table.

"Darn' good. It's a long time since breakfast." He hated that his hand shook as he lifted the cup, and that the woman was watching him out of those pale, observant eyes.

Drugs? she wondered. *Or booze?* Then shook her head in answer to herself. These days what was troubling this man had been given a fancy name that meant nothing. "Post traumatic stress disorder." Why couldn't painful memories be called what they were instead of being disguised? *Call a spade a spade*, she said to herself. *Or a crucifixion. Leave it to Jilly!*

"Where you from?" she asked to break the silence.

He shrugged, hoping she wasn't one of those nosy broads who wanted his entire history. "No place."

"Never been there myself." She grinned. "Oh, don't worry. I'm not a gossip, and I don't pry. A man's business is his own. Just if you feel like talking and not eating alone, I'm a good listener. And this place is my newspaper. I don't get out much, as you can see."

He was ashamed. "Sorry."

"No need."

"These days I talk mostly to myself. It's better that way. No arguments. No insults or discussions that get wrapped around the axle."

"Boring, though, I'll bet." She poured a cup for herself, stirred it, watched the cream swirl in the dark mixture.

He didn't answer. *Safe* was more like it.

Jilly came out with a bowl of black bean soup and a basket of hot fry bread. "Seconds are free," she said, and stared at him with depthless eyes.

Mary Anne had cooked a soup like this once. Mary Anne. He swallowed. *Don't go there.*

The briefest of shadows crossed his face and was gone, but not before Liz saw and recognized it. The funny thing about grief was that, over time, it dissipated. Minutes became hours, then days, and then, suddenly, became the most poignant of memories, recollections of happiness mingled with the pain that had receded to some small place deep within.

You could, of course, prolong the emptiness, lose yourself in pity, anger, and loss, or you could keep going, make friends, forget self, and do for others. In her life she'd done both.

With a quick flick of her wrist, she turned the chair and went back to the counter. Jilly was always warning her about getting involved in someone's problems, and this man was a stranger. A while back everybody had been talking about the ex-marine who'd gunned down the patrons in a restaurant, and, here, there were the illegals who poured across the border—some seeking work, some merely desperate—and the dopers, violent, greedy men who made their money from the suffering of others.

On the advice of Sheriff Willie Budd, she kept a loaded .38 in a drawer, and, although she could nail a rabbit at fifty yards, she hoped she'd never need it for a human.

"Want the last newspaper?" she asked. "It's free."

The soup had mellowed him, and he realized he'd been acting weird, falling into that half crazy state he couldn't seem to avoid. His mother would have scolded him big time. "You be polite, Jack Roman!"

Instead, he'd sloughed off this woman crippled worse than he was but making a life, and with a face that was almost, not quite, beautiful, because he'd been mired in his own swamp. He looked up at Jilly, a dark statue in the kitchen doorway. "I'll take those seconds," he said, "if your offer's still good." To the woman in her chair, he said: "My mom would have blistered my backside for being rude to a lady. Come on back and sit."

"Well that's a relief." She spun around, maneuvered

from behind the counter, and came toward him. "I always think that folks who won't talk have something to hide. Nowadays you can't tell what."

He sighed. If it was talk she wanted, she'd get it. When he was through, he'd go out, get in the truck, and let the silence take him. "So are you from around here?" he asked.

"Born and bred." She pulled closer to the table and picked up her cup, looking into it again as if she could read past and future in its depths. "My grandparents homesteaded here before there was a town. Mom and Dad ranched and added to the place, and I was born in the old house. It's still there." She sighed, remembering. Maybe this man was right. Silence was safe.

He sipped his soup. "And?"

She'd asked for this. "And the polio virus got here a couple years before the vaccine. I was one of the lucky ones, if that's what you want to call it. I survived."

Out on the highway, a semi geared down and rumbled past, shaking the windows. He felt the vibrations, like the words she'd left unspoken, down to his boots. "Jesus," he said. "Jesus."

She smiled. "As Mom used to say . . . 'Jesus had nothing to do with it'."

He didn't want to hear her troubles. His own were burden enough. Still, he'd started this with a simple question, and he figured he might as well keep her talking. "You still own the ranch?"

She toyed with her spoon, amazed that her own fingers trembled. Where had she gone, that young Liz, that girl who rode horses, that child filled with dreaming and innocence? Where had the world, as she'd known it, disappeared?

"Sold it!" Her voice was harsh. "But I couldn't leave here, you know? Here's where I belong. Those mountains out there are mine. The time I spent in the hospital told me that."

He knew about time in hospitals, about the thoughts that swirled in your head, the nightmares, the longing to have everything back as it had been.

Jilly came out with his sandwich, her face solemn. "The young people, they leave here and go to the cities where the money is," she said. "But this place is painted on their hearts. You'll see. You stay, and you'll see."

Jack looked from one woman to the other. What the hell kind of talk was this? He almost felt like she'd cast a spell, and he didn't need any magic, or maybe he did, but he'd be the one to instigate it, not this Indian with her face carved from stone.

He laughed. "If you cook like this all the time, I just might."

"You come for breakfast," she said, still expressionless. "Then you go out and listen to the mountain."

"Quit playing medicine woman," Liz advised with a chuckle. "You'll scare the man." And to Jack: "But what she said is true. When you leave, just stand out there and listen. Leave your windows open when you sleep tonight. You'll hear all the music in the world. Good for the soul."

The sun had gone behind the mountain, and the

miles-long shadow of evening moved like dark water across the valley, up cañons and steep slopes. A street light flickered on, illuminating the store and his truck that seemed abandoned, an isolated shard of another time and place.

He realized he'd been so caught up in talk that he'd forgotten himself, and he wasn't sure he liked the feeling. It left him naked, somehow defenseless, against what he couldn't say.

"Reckon you want to close." He pushed away from the table. "But I'll take you up on breakfast."

"We're open at seven." Liz wheeled back behind the cash register, then glanced up at him. "My name's Liz Jerome. When you go down to the motel, tell Luisa I sent you. Tell her you want the back cabin. It's away from the road."

He put out his hand. "Jack Roman. And thanks for the company, and the advice."

"Any time." She shook his hand briefly, then counted out his change. "I'll lock up after you."

He opened the screen door and went out.

"Wait!" She was close behind. "Do something, will you?"

"What?"

"Stop and listen a minute."

He jammed his hands in his pockets and, humoring her, leaned against one of the wooden posts of the *portal*.

The highway was empty. Above the dark peaks of the mountains a sickle moon carved a piece of sky. Lis-

213

tening, he heard only silence—his own breath, a sudden gust of wind that rattled the door. And then it came, not from one direction but from everywhere, a soft, gentle fluting, a sweetness like honey, a blurred pouring out of indescribable music.

"What?" he asked, startled. "What *is* that?"

Her face shone pale in the street light, a white flower. "Nighthawks," she said. "They sing like that all night now. Maybe mating. Maybe a lullaby. I'm not sure. But that's what I meant before. What Jilly was talking about. It's a comfort, and it's freely given."

"I've never heard anything like that at all," he said, waiting with shoulders hunched for the hunger, the grief to overwhelm him again.

Coming up on San Felipe, Raul debated whether to slow down and observe the speed limit, or blast through and hope no lingering deputy had stopped for coffee at the store of the cripple.

He himself had stopped there often and sat listening to the talk. In his business, he must always listen, cocking an ear to any tidbit of information that might be of use.

The cripple, he thought, was a handsome woman with eyes as unreadable as glass. He'd often wondered what she would be like in his bed. The truck swerved, interrupting the image of the two of them, and he came back to the present with a curse. Thinking about women was for later. Now he would go through San Felipe at top speed, and, if anyone saw, he'd be gone before they could catch him.

The passengers were quiet, sleeping maybe. Good. Out of the corner of his eye he sneaked a look at the girl, her face lit by the green light from the dashboard. In profile she was a slight, slant-eyed Madonna with shadows painted under high cheek bones. A kid, probably no older than his youngest sister, safe at home, an American like him.

Hell, they all wanted to be Americans. That he understood. Life was good here, and the smart ones could make money. Like him. Money was what mattered. With money you could have anything, any woman you wanted.

The lights of San Felipe grew brighter. He accelerated. Beside him the girl stiffened as if protesting the speed.

"Quit worrying," he said to her. "I am Raul. I know what I'm doing."

The truck was coming fast. Jack and Liz watched in horror as a tire blew and shattered, and the truck, out of control, skidded across the road, hit a ditch, and overturned, then slid forward until it crashed against a stone wall.

Instinctively Jack ducked, hearing not the screech of metal, the crunch as the front end crumpled, but the whine of shells . . . women and children screaming . . . the explosion of a grenade almost under his feet. And then silence again, broken only by the *tinkle* of shattered glass, the *hiss* of escaping steam.

He was dying again in the stinking jungle, and, out of reach, Mary Anne, trapped beneath her car, was dying, too. He was helpless, caught in the senseless repetition of a never-ending nightmare.

"Jilly, come quick!" Liz's voice was shrill, her hands clenched in frustration. She hated it! Hated being tied to a padded chair, glued to a set of wheels, and unable to do anything but scream for Jilly.

"I'm here." Jilly was carrying a stack of blankets and a flashlight. "I'll see what I can do. You call Willie Budd and the medics, and make more coffee. This night's gonna be a long one."

Both women looked at Jack, still hunched into himself, his eyes closed, sweat beaded on his forehead.

Jilly said: "Mister Roman, I'm gonna need your help."

Blankly he stared at her out of eyes like flat metal discs. "I can't."

"Yeah, you can. If you don't, you won't be able to look at yourself in the morning. Come on."

She headed across the road, quiet as a shadow in her moccasins, and, step-by-step, he followed, the stink of burnt rubber, hot metal making him want to puke. He didn't have to do this. Didn't want to. Who in hell did she think she was, the crazy woman now shining her flashlight on a bloody, twisted corpse? And what was he doing following her like a pup on a leash? He knew all he needed to know about death and how it happened; he carried the images with him day and night, and they were heavy, like boulders, a constant, bitter curse.

Jilly covered the body with one of the incongruously bright blankets. "A boy," she said, her eyes reflecting the light like foxfire. "He came here with nothing like all the rest. They come with only hope, and they die with that hope dancing down the road in front of them."

He said: "There isn't any hope."

"For them, maybe not. For you . . . you have life. Many years to find your way."

His bitter retort was cut off by a moan from inside the vehicle. Swiftly Jilly went, knelt down, and peered inside, then shook her head. "We can't do anything. She's caught in there . . . with four more. Damn that sheriff! And those medics. Never anywhere when you want them. Go back inside and find out where they are."

"She?" His voice rasped, unsteady. "Is there a woman in there?

"A girl. Chinese, like the boy, I think. Now go do what I said."

He turned slowly. "Chinese?"

"Death isn't picky," she said. "Go now."

The faces were there again, a grotesque collage, a field of slaughter. Only Mary Anne's face as she lay dying eluded him. How long had she lain there before help came, and him waiting for her, happy with the pair of legs that at last supported him. Home! After eighteen months, he was going home! He had paced the lobby, impatient and testing himself. No longer a cripple tied to a bed and a chair, strapped to a gurney on the way to another surgery. Home! And if he still had ghostly, distorted memories of 'Nam, at least he'd be where he belonged.

"Jack." Joel Silverstein had been standing beside him.

"Hey, Doc! Come to kick me out?"

Silverstein had taken his arm. "Come on back to my office a minute, will you?"

He'd gone berserk in that office. It had taken three orderlies to subdue him when the doctor broke the news. "Died on the way to the hospital." He could still hear the voice—quiet, compassionate, lethal.

Except in dreams he'd never seen Mary Anne again. Those dreams, fueled by imagination—of his wife broken and burned beyond recognition, one more victim in the sea of victims who taunted him, screamed their abusive agony—kept him in the hospital another eight months, this time in the psycho ward.

He lurched into the café and stopped, blinded by the light.

"Bad?" Liz's voice was husky.

"One dead. A kid. Five more stuck inside. Where's the medics, for God's sake?"

"On their way. Old man Rabb's been snake bit, and Willie's out some place chasing himself. Too much country, not enough men, or so he says. I hate this, you know! Being helpless. This damned waste. Kids dying in my own yard, and for what? Because they're hungry? Because they think things are better here? Maybe dying is better. Hell, I couldn't even manage that!"

Her misery touched him. There she sat behind the

218

counter, day in and day out, living her life through others. He reached across and put a hand over hers. "Neither could I," he told her. "Neither could I. And the hell of it is, I can't figure out why I even bothered living."

"Tell me about it." She pushed away from his kindness. "Maybe take some water out there . . . and some towels. They're in the back."

"Jilly says they're Chinese."

She looked up, startled. "So far from home. Makes you wonder. Like all the rest, they'll have no identification. Every old graveyard around has a couple headstones marked 'Unnamed Mexican.' It makes you think about whoever's waiting for them to come back. They never do, and we don't even know their names."

"I didn't know names in 'Nam, either," he said. "They were just the enemy."

"And now?"

"Now I can't forget them."

This time she reached out a hand and touched him. "You did what you had to."

"Why, I wonder."

She thought a minute, searching for what she hoped would be the right words. "Because you believed it was right, maybe. I don't know. I really don't. All I do know is that it's done, and you're here, and there's no sense going back over what's finished. I learned that the hard way." Her pale eyes glinted. "I still get mad sometimes. You just saw me. But then I think there's things I have to do. Like right now. You go help Jilly. That's your job.

Maybe it's why you came in here tonight. There's no such thing as coincidence, you know, and, if you don't, ask Jilly. She'll tell you."

"The mill of the gods?" he said, giving her a smile.

"Kind of like that, except her gods aren't what you think. Now go on and don't mind me."

He pushed open the door, and the moths that had come, attracted to the light, flew upward, a thousand wings as fragile as tissue paper, whirling over his head. Out of the darkness of his own despair, he magnified the tragedy of those small lives doomed to death by the very brilliance that had lured them. What was the point? Where was the reason in any passage through the maze of this tragedy called life? Was his mission simply to cross the road and kneel in the dust beside Jilly while waiting for death to arrive?

"What's happened?" A small, dark-haired woman, one of several people who had come out of their houses, grabbed his arm. Couldn't she see? Or did she simply need the sound of a voice, reassurance that death had passed her by?

"Go ask Liz," he said. "Go keep her company."

Was it then that the singing began, or had it started while he stood watching the moths spin their frantic circle? As he crossed the road, he heard it—minor, insistent, hypnotic as a drumbeat, and coming from everywhere like the music of the birds.

Jilly, he saw, was seated on the ground, and the soft chanting rose out of her throat and drifted away, an almost visible melody. He went and sat beside her, avoiding the body hidden under the blanket, turning his eyes away from the crumpled vehicle. "They're on their way," he said.

She seemed not to have heard, was lost in the unintelligible syllables of a song as old as her people, a melding of earth, sky, and spirit, and he let himself go with the rhythm that, like a gentle darning, seemed to be binding up the holes in the torn web that bound them all.

Far away, on the road north, flashing lights appeared. Abruptly Jilly stopped. "It is finished."

He shook himself awake. "What . . . what was that?"

She looked at him, pleased. "It was Nightway. What I remember of it. Too much bad here tonight, so I sang to the Holy People."

Somehow they had come—her gods—out of the dark.

"What were the words?" Still lost in harmony, he needed to hold to the meaning.

She leaned back on her hands and raised her head to the sky that was now littered with stars and began again to chant, this time in a language he understood.

> The world before me is restored in beauty.
> The world behind me is restored in beauty.
> The world below me is restored in beauty.
> The world above me is restored in beauty.
> All things around me are restored in beauty.
> My voice is restored in beauty.
> It is finished in beauty.
> It is finished in beauty.

His troubles were not going to disappear merely because of an ancient chant. He knew that, but, strangely, he felt lighter, and safe, as if a wall had arisen between him and the ghosts that hounded him.

He did not know what form Jilly's gods took, but, as the lights from the approaching ambulance flickered through the trees, he was aware of the mountains that embraced the valley like protecting arms.

"Listen to the mountains," Jilly had told him.

Perhaps he would. Or perhaps they had already spoken their message, and the evil had been vanquished, absorbed into receptive earth.

Inside the truck, the girl lay listening to the music. It sounded to her like the music of water dripping on stone, like the murmur of the river that swirled past her village on its way to the sea. There was darkness, and there was pain, but there was also beauty, even in death.

From the valley, from beneath tall grasses, from out of the very air itself, came the gentle fluting of the birds. She whimpered once, and then slowly, as if to grasp the sound and hold it, she reached out her hand.

Out of the corner of his eye, Jack caught the small gesture and, for a reason he never afterward could explain, reached through the shattered window and took her hand gently in his own.

Acknowledgements

My thanks, as always, to my husband, Glenn Boyer, for his incomparable knowledge of the West and its history, and whose comments on at least one story in this collection saved me from error; to Ben Traywick, the official historian of Tombstone, Arizona for his help and information on the Chinese in Tombstone; to Sinclair Browning, Diane Balinoff, John Duncklee, and Dean Nelson for their advice on driving horse herds; and to my agent, Jon Tuska, for his constant encouragement and wonderful sense of humor. *Abeo, abeo, abeo, actum est, comites!*

Center Point Publishing
600 Brooks Road ● PO Box 1
Thorndike ME 04986-0001 USA

(207) 568-3717

US & Canada:
1 800 929-9108